Return to Turtle Beach

Richard Clark

Praise for Richard Clark's Books

'Clark is particularly good on the colours, flavours and scents of Greece. He has got under the skin of the place in a way few outsiders have been able to.'
Mark Hudson, winner of *Somerset Maugham Award, Thomas Cook Travel Book Award, Samuel Johnson Prize*

Richard Clark captures the spirit of Greece I love. His books make me long to see the places he describes.'
Jennifer Barclay, author of *Falling in Honey* and *An Octopus in My Ouzo*

'There is poetry in Richard Clark's words and through his eyes. I recommend anyone missing Greece, visiting Greece or just wishing they could go to Greece to take a look!'
Sara Alexi, author of *The Greek Village Series*

'Thanks, Richard, for adding your great eye to your gifted pen in service to sharing the essence of Greece with the world!'
Jeffrey Siger, bestselling, award-winning US crime writer

'Richard Clark writes with great authority and a deep affection for his subject, which comes from his long association with Greece… excellent.'

Marjory McGinn, author of *Things Can Only Get Feta, Homer's Where the Heart Is, A Scorpion in the Lemon Tree* and *A Saint for the Summer*

This beautiful story (*The Lost Lyra*) will renew your faith in mankind and make you believe in fate.

Maria A. Karamitsos, founder and editor, *Windy City Greek*

By the Same Author

The Greek Islands – A Notebook

Crete – A Notebook

Rhodes – A Notebook

Corfu – A Notebook

Hidden Crete – A Notebook

More Hidden Crete – A Notebook

Eastern Crete – A Notebook

Richard Clark's Greek Islands Anthology

The Crete Trilogy

The Lost Lyra

ISBN – 13:9781656955449

www.facebook.com/richardclarkbooks

https://notesfromgreece.com

About the Author

Richard Clark is a writer, editor and journalist who has worked on an array of national newspapers and magazines in the UK. In 1982, on a whim, he decided to up sticks and live on the Greek island of Crete. So began a love affair that has continued to this day, and he still visits the Greek islands, where he has a home, on a regular basis. In 2016, he gave up the daily commute to London to become a full-time author. He is married with two grown up children and three grandchildren, and lives in Kent.

Acknowledgements

This book is a work of fiction. Although based on real places in Crete several locations are the product of my imagination alone and all characters are fictitious. Any mistakes are mine.

Once again I owe a debt of gratitude to Tony and Bernadette Prouse for reading each chapter as it was written and guiding me in the right direction. Similarly, a huge thank you goes to the author Yvonne Payne for reading and giving her comments on the final manuscript.

It would be remiss not to thank my great editor Jennifer Barclay and cover designer Mike Parsons, both of whom have worked tirelessly to bring *Return to Turtle Beach* to fruition. Finally, I would like to thank my family, Denise, Rebecca, James, Pete, Lucy, Esther, Imogen and Iris for being so supportive in every way.

Note

The names of male Greek characters ending in an 's' will drop the letter in the vocative case (when that character is being addressed in direct speech).

This book is a work of fiction. All the characters, names and events are the product of the author's imagination and any resemblance to real persons, living or dead, is purely coincidental.

For Iris

Chapter 1

THIS HAD BEEN their secret place. From the mountainside, Popi's head span as she looked down the vertiginous rock face that fell towards the sandy bay far below. Confused and dizzy, she found it impossible to anchor her thoughts about her father. She had last seen him alive ten years ago. Now he lay buried in the cemetery up the mountain, her final memory of him a face at peace staring from the open coffin that morning.

She longed to get down to the beach but it was impossible to reach, except by boat. She knew she should return to the *makaria* meal held to celebrate her father but was struggling to regain composure. The sight of his kindly face in death and the affection with which he was mourned had eased the resentful feeling of abandonment she had built up over the years since her parents' separation.

Now the mist of her memories of their last day together, before she had left Crete for a new life in England, was being wiped clear. She remembered herself as a 13-year-old girl on the beach below, her father saying he would always love her and that some day she might find a way to forgive him. Now she recalled, on that day she had felt nothing but love for the man who had nurtured her all her life, and was broken-hearted that they were being separated. How had time eroded those sentiments? The feelings she had all those years ago now seeming as distant as the sands below.

In the glare of the Cretan spring sunshine her tears began to fall. For so long she had dreamed of returning home. But not like this. Not to bury the father she now knew she had ached to see again. Her mother had not set her against him, but the coldness, the detachment and the sense of loss had, over the years, turned her love to resentment. The sight of the bay glinting in the sun dragged flashbacks of those times to the forefront of her memory.

She had become an inadvertent member of the diaspora, caught up in her mother's need to provide for them both. During her years of exile, thoughts of her father and the island had blurred. It had taken coming here to remember. Now it was too late for them to be reconciled.

The beach was a special place that they shared. As a young girl, Popi had been sworn to secrecy by her dad. He had told her no one must know about their hidden cove. It belonged to the turtles. He had explained that it was where loggerheads came to lay their eggs in the summertime and in years to come the babies born there would return to that same spot to spawn. If the beach was discovered and the tourists came, the eggs would be trampled and the hatchlings never make it to the sea.

Reluctantly she turned her back on the endless blue unrolling its way to the horizon. She must return to the village and the meal to honour her father. Making her way to where she had parked her hire car, the warmth of the spring sun on her skin and the scent of wild mountain herbs helped her regain composure. Looking in the rear-view mirror she checked her face and set off down the mountain road.

As she re-entered the taverna, for a second the room went silent. The quiet moment was almost imperceptible, but in Popi's heightened state she sensed she had been missed. Looking round at the sea of faces there were few she recognised, but they all seemed to know who she was.

The previous afternoon, her flight had landed at Heraklion airport where she picked up her car and headed east to the village. She had never driven in Greece before. Gripping the steering wheel

3

hard, Popi struggled to contain the grief, stress and tiredness she felt as she joined the main road heading in the direction of Agios Nikolaos. The road sped past Malia and began to climb a spectacular gorge between the mountains of Fonia Detis to the south and the sheer rock face of Anavlohos, a commanding barrier between Selinari and the sea.

Near the top of the gorge she made out a tiered tower rising through the trees which struck a chord from her past. A road sign jogged her memory. She slowed and pulled over into the lay-by beneath the steps which led up to the monastery of Agios Georgios, Selinari. Above the arched entrance she could make out the emblem of a two-headed eagle holding an orb and sceptre, the symbol of the Orthodox Church, flanked by two strutting peacocks.

The sight of the monastery reminded her of times she had visited Heraklion with her parents. Her father had always stopped here. He told her Georgios was the saint of travellers, and that not to pay his respects would bring bad luck. He said that when he reached here, he knew he was coming back home. As Popi sat in the driver's seat and drew the sign of the cross over her heart she felt the anxiety drain from her body.

From here she knew it was less than half an hour to the village. She pressed her foot to the floor and the car sped through the groves of olives and orchards of almond trees, past the shells of disused

4

windmills and villages nestling on the mountainside. On the outskirts of Agios Nikolaos she turned onto the road which skirted the back of the city before climbing the cliffs looking down on the bay of Mirabello.

As the car puffed and panted towards the summit, her mind flashed back all those years and she knew what awaited her. Cresting the mountain above Lenika, the view across the bay to the canal and beyond towards Spinalonga was breathtaking. The sea was like a mirror, not a whisper of wind creased its mercury-like face. But Popi recalled days when those waters would heave and sigh and the small fishing boats would run for the narrow canal which linked Mirabello with the more sheltered bay of Korfos.

The road dropped down to sea level, narrowing to pass between the shops and tavernas which announced her arrival in Elounda. She had to concentrate hard to navigate among the parked cars and oncoming traffic and pedestrians walking in the road. Popi followed the one-way system along the quayside onto the road which led back into the hills and the village.

Despite being away for almost half her lifetime Popi felt the strange comfort of homecoming, a belonging which had always been absent in England, although she liked her adopted homeland well enough. Somehow Crete seemed to fit her, she was part of it. In Salisbury, even as she walked the vast expanse of the Plain, she felt herself an observer. When she went to Plymouth to study for her degree in marine biology, although she felt the pull of the sea, there was a brooding undercurrent beneath its oily surface which made her wary. She had enjoyed university life, and had been a good student, but she had never felt quite part of things.

In the years since they had left Crete, Popi's mother had transferred her nursing skills to the hospital in the English city and worked hard to make a living for them there. They settled in a rented cottage in sight of the spectacular cathedral spire, the tallest in the country which had dominated that spot since the 13th century.

Life had been tough for Katerina, a single mother in a foreign land, and she had put all her energies into building a decent future for the daughter she so doted on. It was only when Popi had secured a place to study at university that her mother found a bit of time to indulge herself. Even then, in the beginning, Katerina struggled to adjust to her daughter's absence from home.

It was in her second year at university that Popi noticed a gradual change in her mother as she settled down in her student bedsit to enjoy their nightly telephone conversations. The anxiety in her mother's questioning about her days had abated and Popi picked up on her lightened mood.

When Popi returned home for the Easter break, she discovered the source of her mother's happiness. Arriving tired after her three-hour train journey, she was fumbling for her key when the front door of the cottage was flung open by her smiling mother. She could not remember Katerina looking so radiant. As she stood aside to let her daughter pass into the small sitting room, a smiling man rose from the sofa to his full height and, bending slightly, offered his hand to Popi. Katerina was like a nervous schoolgirl introducing her first boyfriend to her parents. Popi could not suppress a smile.

'This is my friend Andrew. He works with me at the hospital,' her mother gushed.

Popi's hug told her mother there was no need for explanations. She was formally introduced to the engaging radiologist. In no time at all Popi could see why this kind, open man had found his way into her mother's affections.

If her mother had found happiness with Andrew, Popi was finding love more elusive. She had been asked out on dates on numerous occasions at university. She even went out on some, but her romances had been short-lived. For some reason she found it difficult to make a connection with the men she met. Always there was this nagging doubt that any relationship would not last, so it was best to end things before they got too serious.

The Cretan darkness was falling as she parked her car outside the church and dragged her stroller case through the wild daisies, poppies and geraniums which had encroached on the path leading to

7

the main lane of the village. As she approached the still familiar entrance to the home she had once shared with her parents she was met by the warm embraces of her aunt and uncle whose smiling faces she recognised instantly, even after all their years apart. They ushered her inside the house to where her father lay at rest in his coffin on the large kitchen table she remembered sitting around with him and her mother.

Then, unexpectedly, reality hit her, the sense of loss at seeing her father in death. If she thought time had cooled the love she felt for him, this tsunami of grief proved how fine the sands were beneath which her emotions had been buried.

Her aunt, her father's sister, provided the shoulder Popi needed to cry on. As the squall of her anguish abated, her uncle led the two women out to the courtyard garden. The evening was redolent with the soothing scents of the bougainvillea which overhung the table at which they sat and the wild herbs that flourished on the slopes of the mountains that hugged the village. In the light of candle lanterns set by her uncle on the crumbling stone wall, Popi could make out the magnificent display of geraniums of all hues which erupted from impromptu containers, olive oil tins, old tyres, a discarded sink.

'Manolis loved this garden. He was taken from us too young. Fifty-two is no age to die.' Her uncle placed glasses and a small carafe of clear liquid and a jug of wine on the table.

8

Pouring two glasses of raki, he slid one across the table towards Popi.

'*Yamas*, cheers. To Manolis. The best of men.'

Popi raised her glass and drank as she had seen her father do in the kafenio when she was a small girl. She coughed a little as the spirit caught her throat before warming her stomach.

'To father.' Popi responded before placing her glass back on the table and accepting a glass of wine from her aunt.

She had fond childhood memories of her father's younger sister, Thea, and her husband Spyros. To her they had changed little in the intervening years. They had welcomed her back as if it had been only yesterday that she had been playing hide and seek in their olive grove just above the village.

'Welcome home, Popi. I wish your return could have been in better circumstances. How is your mum?' Thea asked.

Looking down the mountains across the starlit waters of the bay, they fell into conversation about Popi's time in England and life in the village since she had left 10 years earlier. As they talked, her aunt went back inside the house, returning with plates of mezzes: meatballs in ouzo, Cretan sausage, haricot beans baked in tomatoes and onion, vine leaves stuffed with mint and rice… The smell of the delicious food mingled with the scents of the early-blooming flowers and the aroma of the mountain herbs, the only sounds those of their voices and the occasional tinkling of goat bells somewhere in the hills above.

From the conversation, Popi got a very different picture of the man who was her father from the one she had painted in her head. Although the loss of his business had hit him hard and, devastated by the loss of his wife and daughter, for a short time he had taken to drink, with the help of other family and friends he had managed to rebuild his life. He had found enough work in the boatyards of Agios Nikolaos to keep body and soul together, had stopped drinking and found solace in the simple life of the village. He had not died destitute, a fear Popi had when she received news of her father's death. Although premature, the heart attack which took him, her aunt and uncle assured her, had deprived this world of a man who had discovered contentment. He had collapsed in the very garden they were sitting in, while watering his plants.

As they talked, Popi could sense the respect and love felt towards her father by the communtiy. When her aunt and uncle excused themselves to go and replenish the table, she walked to the boundary wall and stared down on the twinkling lights of Elounda. Just a 20-minute walk away down the donkey track which led from the village, tourists would be enjoying their holidays, eating and drinking in the tavernas and cafes which skirted the waterfront of the pretty seaside town. Beyond lay the deep blue of the bay of Korfos against the silhouetted backdrop of the hills on Kalidon, the canal-side lights of a taverna marking the spot where a bridge anchored it to the mainland.

She stepped down from the terrace onto the scrubland to the side of the house. Peering into the darkness she could make out the grove of olive trees spreading into the mountains beyond. The peace she felt was like nothing she could remember having experienced. Her reverie was halted as her eyes fell across a strange skeletal object on the grass beneath the trees. It reminded her of the bones of a blue whale she had seen some years ago on a visit to London's Natural History Museum.

'The caique, you've found it.' Popi started at her uncle's voice behind her. 'Since we brought it up here your dad never could find it within himself to let it go, although it was the source of so many of his troubles.'

As her eyes adjusted to the dark, Popi could make out the keel, ribs and frame of a boat. It must have been 10 metres in length.

'Your father and I towed it up here on a trailer when he lost his yard.' Spyros sensed his niece's amazement at seeing the boat half way up a mountain.

'What you'll do with it now I don't know.'

Popi turned to face her uncle, his smiling face illuminated by a garden light. 'It's all yours now. Your father was determined that you should inherit everything.'

'He loved you, Popi. He didn't think it amounted to much, but there's the house, the land, his car and scooter and the olive trees and…' Her uncle gestured towards the skeleton of the boat.

Speechless, Popi allowed herself to be led by the hand back to the terrace. It had never occurred to her that she would be the beneficiary of her father's estate. Sitting back down, she listened again to her aunt and uncle reminiscing about her dad. Slowly she gained a picture of the true nature of her father, rather than the one imagined in her years of estrangement. The renewed flood of tears was testament to the wave of grief for her father's passing that swamped her.

With the funeral the next day, Popi tried to get some sleep. As she lay on top of her old childhood bed she restlessly tried to make sense of all that had happened. Their separation had eroded the memories of the happy times. Regaining the clarity of the love she felt for her father made her grief all the harder to bear.

She was awoken by a knock on the bedroom door.

'Would you like breakfast outside on your terrace?' her aunt asked, smiling. 'The undertakers are arriving in two hours. I thought you'd like me to wake you.'

12

Popi was nursed into the day by a breakfast of coffee, fruit, yoghurt and honey laid out for her on the table outside. She forced herself to eat, but even the stunning view across the bay could not unravel the knots which she felt in her stomach at the prospect of the day's events.

*

After the funeral, the sealed coffin was lowered into the earth of the cemetery on the hill above the village. The mourners lay flowers on the grave, while the slightest of breezes ruffled the silver leaves of the sea of olive trees cascading down to the bay below. Blood red poppies and pure white daisies dotted the parched ground, and as Popi looked up from the open grave to the view across the bay she could not imagine a spot closer to heaven on earth.

As they gathered for the *makaria* meal, the village taverna was packed. Its windows had been thrown open to give relief from the searing heat coming off the grill, and tables and chairs had been put outside to accommodate the guests who wanted to mark Manolis' passing. Popi had never been very comfortable in crowds, and the melee as she entered augmented the tiredness and grief that swept over her. She felt her pulse begin to race. Her breathing quickened as beads of perspiration broke out on her forehead.

'Are you alright?' Thea sensed her niece's distress.

13

'I'll be fine, I just need to get some air.' Popi pushed through the throng to the door, reaching in her bag for the car keys.

As she walked along the village lanes she tried to slow her breathing, and by the time she reached the vehicle her anxiety was subsiding. Sitting in the car, she opened the windows and contemplated what to do. She was not yet ready to face all those people. She needed a quiet place where she could get a grip of her feelings. Suddenly it came to her where she should go.

Her memory served her well and she easily found the spot. Pulling the car over then walking to the cliff edge high above the horseshoe cove. Sitting on the warm earth, the only thing to interrupt her thoughts was the buzzing of cicadas. As she stared down at the secret place, it began to work its magic. Catching sight of the hidden cove was like unearthing the good memories of her dad, which had somehow got buried beneath the sands of time. Now her father was at rest on the mountain above the bay. Looking down on this special place she had shared with him, memories of those times brought a smile to Popi's face.

Back at the taverna, Popi was surprised at how relaxed she now felt. In England she had often been uncomfortable at large gatherings, even in the company of people she knew. As she took her seat next to Spyros and Thea, she sensed the wine and raki had eased any previous formality among the gathering. Gradually guests

14

introduced themselves. With her uncle there to aid her memory, some she could place in the complicated jigsaw of her past which she was piecing together in her mind.

School friends, some with partners, and even children; neighbours; shopkeepers; fishermen all stirred recollections, clearing the amnesia induced by years of absence. The friendly welcome and the food and drink made it difficult for the earlier disquiet to re-establish itself. The tide had turned from reverential to celebratory. Somewhere a lyra struck up and the voices in the room rose to compete with the haunting melodies.

'This is what your dad would have wanted,' Spyros shouted. 'And as you can see, he was much loved.'

'Good' and 'kind' were words which kept cropping up as guests approached Popi to convey their condolences. She was grateful those sentiments reinforced what she had felt earlier looking down on Turtle Beach. Now she was back in Crete, she wondered how she ever let the years make her indifferent to her love for her dad.

It was late by the time an exhausted Popi, Thea and Spyros made their excuses and walked up the hillside path back to Manolis' house. Although she was tired, Popi's head was swirling with the events of the day. She suggested they sit out on the terrace and drink a coffee. Her aunt headed to the kitchen, casting aside protests from Popi that she would make the drinks.

'You go and sit, I will join you in a minute.'

Spyros ushered Popi outside onto the terrace, taking a bottle of Metaxa and three glasses from the sideboard. As he poured the brandy, the sound of the lyra and voices of last guests wafted up the mountainside. Far below in Elounda the lights twinkled as though reflecting the abundance of stars in the clearest of skies.

'It was a fitting send off. Your father would have approved.' Spyros raised his glass.

'To Manolis. The best of men.'

'To Dad. May you rest in peace.' Popi's whisper echoed the toast to the man she had only today begun to find a way to reconnect with. Somewhere in her mind it troubled her that on hearing of her father's death she had travelled to Crete out of a sense of duty. Already it was apparent that her feelings ran much deeper than that. Popi sat letting her thoughts and the distant strains of the music wash over her.

'Costa, are you alright, it's very late?' From inside they heard Thea's voice. 'Come in, would you like coffee? We're sitting on the terrace.'

'I am sorry to disturb you so late.' Popi recognised something in the tall young man now filling the doorway which led out onto the terrace. But I felt I had to come.'

16

'Come, come Costa, *katse*, sit. You know Popi.' Spyros welcomed the unexpected guest.

'You remember Costas, your father's apprentice when he had the business?'

In her mind Popi stripped 10 years away from the muscular, long-haired man who stood before her and tried to reconcile it with her memory of a skinny, shy lad who her father had taken on to learn his trade.

She stood, smiling. 'Of course I remember, Costa, please sit down.'

'Thank you. I will not stay long. It is so late. I had to work today so miss the funeral. I'm sorry but I wanted to pay my respects.'

'Thank you for coming. Would you like a Metaxa?' Popi stood to get him a glass.

'No, thank you. Thea has offered me a coffee, and I have to drive back to Agios Nikolaos tonight.'

As Thea arrived with a tray of coffees and glasses of water, Spyros tried to engage Costas in conversation. Although he had made the late-evening journey from the town to give his condolences to the family, the young man appeared embarrassed and reluctant to talk. For Popi, sensing his discomfiture, it was a relief when Costas finished his coffee and stood to leave.

'I appreciate your visit Costa; it was good to meet again after all this time. Will I see you before I go back to England?'

'I don't know. I live in Agios Nikolaos now, and it is a busy time for me. Owners want their boats ready for the summer, so I am working long hours. Goodbye, and sorry again for the lateness of my visit.' Backing through the door as Popi stood, he said, 'I'll see myself out.'

'Well that was a surprise,' said Thea. 'It's not often we see Costas around here these days.'

'I think he found it tough when your father had to let him go when the business folded. I have to say I'm surprised he came.' Spyros explained.

'It must have been hard, particularly during this recession,' Popi found some sympathy for Costas' position.

'Sometimes I bump into him if I go to Agios on business, but he always appears to want to get away quickly. If he realised how much it had hurt your father to lose the business and have to curtail his apprenticeship, perhaps he would stop being so resentful. Your dad said he showed a lot of promise as a craftsman. His skills are definitely wasted working on the plastic boats in the marina but that's life.' Spyros poured himself another measure.

Popi held a hand over her glass. 'No more for me, I'll only suffer in the morning if I do. I suppose we have much to sort out?'

'There's no rush. When do you return to England?'

'I haven't a set date. I took compassionate leave from my job at the university, so I have until September before I need to get back. I thought I might use the opportunity to take a break.' Popi realised her aunt and uncle knew little about her life in England.

'I stayed on at university after I graduated. I'm a marine biologist and work as a junior lecturer and do research.'

'You're a woman of the sea, you followed in your father's footsteps.' Thea smiled.

'I love the fieldwork, though I don't get out as much as I would like. I do spend a lot of time on boats, but it's a bit colder in Plymouth.'

'Tomorrow we should go back to our house. You are welcome there, or you can stay here if you don't mind being alone.' Spyros rose from his chair. 'But that can wait 'til the morning. I must go to bed.'

Thea rose to join her husband. '*Kalinichta*, goodnight.'

Left alone on the terrace, Popi closed her eyes. The slightest of warm breezes took the edge off the heat of the spring night and the silence sang to her soul. Looking up, the stars floated on a sea of sky. She felt tiny in the face of this vast universe and comfortable in her place on earth. The ghosts of the past in the house did not haunt her. If she could, she would stay here.

Chapter 2

THE WAKE OF a small boat heading for the canal was the only thing which ruffled the calm of the early morning sea. Inside Manolis was in turmoil, his grip on the tiller firmer than the caress he usually used to coax the workboat onto its course. On the foredeck he looked at the young girl coiling the mooring rope as she had done so many times before. He turned aft and wiped a solitary tear from his eye.

How had it come to this? At sea he had faced the fiercest of weather, always finding a way to navigate safely back to harbour. Onshore his life had hit the rocks and now he was losing the two people he loved most in the world. For some time he had known that his relationship with Katerina was foundering as wave after wave of misfortune threatened the stability of their lives. Somehow Manolis had always thought the tide of their luck would turn and they would emerge the other side ready to sail on through the calmer waters of the future.

Now Manolis knew his marriage was over. The night before, his wife had told him she had got a nursing job in England, 'a country where they pay people so they can afford to feed their children'. She was taking Popi and leaving the country for good. He had no answer; the fates which had conspired against him had left Manolis a broken man. In the eye of the storm which battered their lives he had been unable to steer a way through and had sought refuge in the haven of the local kafenio.

Before, when their lives had cut up rough, one or other of them had been able to provide the anchor to help them cope in choppy waters. This time it appeared their love had not been strong enough to survive the financial hardships and Manolis' escape into drink. At the end of an evening, through the bottom of his empty glass, the boatbuilder knew his drinking was not helping to rescue his family from destitution. But he no longer had the strength to pass by the bar on his way home from his ailing business and take the mountain path back to his wife and daughter.

Ever since Popi had been able to walk, Manolis had delighted in taking his daughter to sea. She in turn loved the freedom of being in the open air. She grew confident on and around boats and spent time in her father's yard at every available opportunity. As she grew older, she would help him paint the hulls of the boats drawn up out of the water and had started to learn the basic skills of a boatbuilder's craft.

Even Popi had noticed the downturn in her father's business. Before this latest commission to build a caique had come through, it had been some time since a boat had emerged from beneath the makeshift tarpaulin staked out on the shoreline. Without a boat to build, she had noticed a change in her father's mood. She no longer heard him humming as he worked. The routine maintenance of his friends' boats kept some money coming in but it was not what her father lived for. He thrived on the chiselling, planing and bending the wood out of which he created the vessels, all different but each one with the most exquisite lines. She shared his pride when a boat was launched into the water and moored up ready for its final fitting out. She had noticed an upturn in his mood when, some months before, he had taken an order for a new caique from a businessman wanting to set up boat trips for the burgeoning tourist market.

The commission had come just in time. Manolis was under pressure as the local government was intent on replacing ailing businesses and renting out the prime waterfront land to more lucrative restaurants and bars. Putting up rents and inventing new restrictions on the land use on a monthly basis, the authorities were unscrupulous in trying to drive off businesses which for centuries had plied their trade on the shores of the bay.

Was it not enough that for years the government had been paying fishermen to bulldoze and burn their boats to help them meet reduced fishing quotas? Tourism was seen by many politicians as the only game in town, the sole way they could extricate the stricken country from the financial mess they had put it in. The fishermen around these parts were luckier than some in that the island of Spinalonga was growing as a tourist attraction. The island saw thousands of visitors daily wanting to take boats to the old leper colony from Elounda or the village of Plaka. Even with this jewel in Crete's crown on their doorstep, the tourist trade was not sufficient to provide all the boat skippers and their crews with a living wage.

Building the new boat would keep the wolves from the door for a few years more, and Manolis borrowed heavily from the bank to buy the wood, paint, chandlery and the engine needed to fulfil the order. With that order now cancelled, the boatbuilder was heavily in debt and bankrupt. His drinking was only making things worse. With Katerina's salary irregular as the state could not afford to pay hospital staff in the face of the financial crisis, the pressure breached the dam of their resilience. Their contentment was overwhelmed with anxiety, which soon turned to acrimony.

As he steered a course towards the narrow canal that linked the bay of Korfos with the waters of Mirabello, Manolis tried to push from his mind the possibility that this might be his last time at sea with his daughter. He had lost his wife, business and self-respect and now he had to tell Popi that she too would be leaving. However much he ached for her to stay, he knew she had to go with her mother. He had no money and, in his more sober moments, he knew in his heart that he could not provide for her.

Easing the boat between the two poles that marked the channel, he steered under the bridge and through the remains of the piers of the old crossing. As they passed into the open sea, he was reminded of the days he had spent anchored here as Popi dived down exploring the remains of the ancient city of Olous which lay beneath the surface. He had always found this connection with the past reassuring, knowing people had lived here since Minoan times. It made him feel safe that he was rooted to this place and its history. Now he could not have felt less secure. His whole world was breaking apart, and somehow he had to tell his child she would be leaving him, maybe forever.

In happier times he had told his daughter how these waters had been the playground of the mermaid goddess Britomartis, the daughter of Zeus who threw herself into the sea to escape the attentions of King Minos. Caught in the nets of fishermen she was rescued and given refuge, and as an act of gratitude had ever since been the protector of seafarers in these parts. But in the dark corners of Manolis' mind he knew there was no rescue from the crisis in which he found himself.

The canal astern, Manolis swung the helm over and steered a course seaward, his boat rising and falling on the slight swell of the open water. Popi lay on the foredeck, the early sun already warm enough to dry the droplets of spray thrown up by the pitch of the boat. It was hard not to feel happy, but she sensed something was wrong with her father. By embracing the warmth and beauty the day had to offer she hoped she could shine light on the darkness she perceived inside her dad.

As the boat approached the cove, Popi made ready the lines while her father cut the engine and bent to the oars, pulling out a course for the rocky promontory at the edge of the bay. She went astern to drop anchor before returning to the bow. Diving into the clear water, she shivered slightly as her body adjusted to the temperature. Swimming the mooring rope ashore, she secured it to a rock as she had so many times before.

For as long as Popi could remember her father had brought her here. He would tell his daughter the story of the caretta caretta, the loggerhead turtles, and how they were endangered and that they must do everything they could to protect them. Pollution and fishing

25

nets were a constant danger in the waters in which the loggerheads swam, and tourism posed a threat on the beaches where they laid their eggs. At this time of year Popi and her father would remain on the rocky arms which encircled the sandy cove, not venturing onto the beach for fear of disturbing the sands. Beneath those sands baby turtles would hatch, waiting until the cool of the night before emerging, and under the cover of darkness attempt their hazardous journey to the sea.

The young loggerheads which made it that far would then drift amongst the seaweed until they grew big enough to swim further afield. In adulthood the turtles could venture more than 10,000 km away from the beach on which they were born, but every two or three years a mature female would return there to lay her own eggs.

Her father had impressed on her that she must keep the cove their secret. He had made her promise not to tell anyone about the beach so that the turtles could continue to lay their eggs in a protected environment. Keeping that promise could not have been easier for Popi, who had seen magnificent adult loggerheads swimming in the bays of Korfos and Mirabello and was determined to do what she could to save these endangered creatures.

That day, unusually, the turtles were not in the forefront of her mind. Behind her father's dull eyes she could sense the battle raging within him. She had caught a sense of his vulnerability and it

26

frightened her. What was it casting a shade of gloom over her dad as they sat in silence staring out towards where the blue of the sea met a cloudless sky?

Manolis could not find in his head the words to soften the blow of what he was about to tell his daughter but he knew he had to say something. He took a deep breath and just let the words tumble out as he exhaled.

'Your mum and I are splitting up. Tomorrow you are moving with her to England.'

'I'm sorry, I don't know how else to tell you.'

*

He turned from her but she caught him wiping his hand across his eyes. She was too shocked to cry but the sight of her strong father so exposed broke her heart.

Although only 13-years-old, she put a comforting arm round his broad shoulders as he told her that he would always love her and was sorry that things had ended up this way and prayed that she could forgive him.

Back in the village her father sought solace in the kafenio as Katerina bustled around the house packing for their trip. Spyros and Thea arrived to lend a hand and promised to package up anything they could not take and get it shipped to England when they had a

27

permanent address. They had always loved Manolis' wife and daughter and were determined not to take sides in the break-up.

*

The excitement of flying for the first time as their plane took off from Heraklion airport the next day pushed the pain to the back of Popi's mind. As the aircraft climbed, the sky was crystal clear and she looked down on the tiny islands floating on the ultramarine Aegean below. She wondered at the snow-capped peaks of the Alps as they crossed from Italy to Switzerland and on into Germany and France before catching glimpses of the English Channel through the clouds as they began their descent into London's Gatwick airport.

Rain streaked the cabin windows when the plane finally emerged from the cloud cover as it made its final approach. Popi's first view of what was to be her new home was of green fields spanned by busy roads and dotted with huge car parks seen through a veil of rain. She couldn't believe the size of the busy airport as they taxied to a jetty and disembarked straight into a corridor which led to the airline terminal.

Somehow they found the train to London before changing to make the journey to Salisbury. By the time they had settled into the room they had rented in a bed-and-breakfast and been to find some food in the city, it was dark. Exhausted, both mother and daughter collapsed into their beds. But sleep didn't come easily. The room, the town, the country… everything around her was strange. As she lay in a strange bed in a strange country, the rain running down the windows muffled her sobs as the full weight of what had happened hit her.

It seemed as though she was cast adrift on a sea of unfamiliarity without the comfort of a safe haven in sight. Although surrounded by buildings and people, she had never felt so alone in the world. She knew she must keep strong for her mother, but her solitude felt absolute and her tears threatened to overwhelm her.

In her bed on the other side of the room, Katerina was also gripped with anxiety. She had to make this work for the sake of her daughter. There was nothing left for her in Crete, her marriage smashed on the rocks of despair brought about by forces beyond her control. The reckless ineptitude and greed of the people who ruled her country and the punitive cruelty of the nation's creditors had stolen her future. If Manolis had not turned to drink and she too readily to exhausted anger, perhaps they could have weathered the storm and salvaged something from their marriage.

The sound of her daughter crying jolted Katerina back to the present. Crossing the room, she engulfed her child in her arms until Popi's tears soaked through her nightdress to her skin. From somewhere Katerina managed to find words of reassurance. As she lay down beside her daughter, soothing her to sleep, she knew she had to stay strong.

*

A good and compassionate nurse, Katerina adjusted to life in an English hospital more quickly than she had expected. The staff made her welcome and although the work was hard, at least she was getting paid. With the small amount of savings she had brought with her, she scraped together enough for the deposit on a small rented house which she set about turning into a home for herself and her child. She worked wonders on her meagre wages. When Popi was not at school and she was not working, they scoured charity shops for furnishings and trinkets to turn the old stone cottage into a cosy retreat.

Some days they would set out early, packing a lunch, and catch a bus out of the city to Old Sarum, Stonehenge or up onto Salisbury Plain. Walking the chalk hills gave them space to relax from the pressures of adjusting to a life far away from Crete. The gently undulating cornfields and wildflower meadows crossed by babbling brooks and chortling streams proved a balm which soothed their homesickness.

By the time Katerina had managed to save enough money to buy a second-hand car, the pull of the sea took them further afield to Lymington, Christchurch and the Beaulieu River. Popi loved being surrounded by boats and could sit for hours watching the comings and goings of yachts in the harbours. Although she felt the open water tug at something in her soul, she still felt like a spectator rather than being a part of this new world in which she was living.

The English Popi had learned in Crete had served her well and had soon been refined into a fluency which helped her settle into the local school. She found her studies helped fend off the loneliness she felt when she was apart from her mother and she proved to be an able student. By the time she had to choose her A-level options she had already decided she wanted to be a marine biologist. A love of the sea and a desire to protect the animals and plants that lived in its depths was rooted deep inside her.

Popi was an accomplished swimmer and when she took her first scuba diving course she found the experience liberating. She was a natural aboard boats, and at university grabbed every opportunity to get out to sea and do fieldwork. In or on the water she somehow felt a connection which was absent in her day-to-day life.

As her adolescent years went by, Popi thought less and less about her childhood. Occasionally thoughts of her father would surface before sinking again into some dark corner of her brain. Protective, Popi and her mother both sought to shield each other from the past, afraid of what spirits such memories might unleash.

Although kept alive in her daytime thoughts and night-time dreams, over the years away from her homeland, Popi's memories of her life there faded. The distance between those days and her life in England in both miles and years had blurred the images of the past. Despite this, at times she felt an ethereal attraction towards Crete, as though being pulled in that direction by an invisible thread. She knew someday she needed to return but when, she didn't know.

As far as Popi knew there had been little contact between her mother and father since they separated. He had sent her a card through her mum every name day, his upset at their estrangement still evident in the simple *agapi Bampa*, 'love Dad', with which he signed the missives. Most of her mother's discussions concerning the divorce had taken place through lawyers and the only contact she still had with her past life was with Uncle Spyros and Aunt Thea, with whom Katerina had been close.

Popi had been at work at the university when her mother had called, informing her of her father's death. Spyros had phoned from Crete to say Manolis had died of a heart attack that afternoon and that the funeral would be held in two days' time. Katerina told her daughter she did not think it appropriate for her to go after the acrimony of their divorce but felt that Popi should get there if at all possible, as she might regret not saying a final farewell to her father.

Popi took a snap decision. She had always valued her mother's counsel and after hanging up the phone, she opened her laptop to see if the journey would be possible. She felt strangely focused as she set her mind to organising the trip. Her lack of grief took her by surprise as she made her travel arrangements. She phoned her department head, who was sympathetic and offered her as much compassionate leave as she needed. She found a flight online that left Gatwick early the following morning. If she hurried she could get a train from Plymouth to Gatwick via Reading, the five-hour journey arriving at the airport in the early hours in time to check in.

Stuffing her hand luggage with the darkest dress she could find, her wash bag and a change of clothes she called a taxi to take her to the station, stopping off at a cash point for some money, she could withdraw euros when she was in Crete. On the train she searched the car hire companies and managed to book a rental she could pick up from the airport.

It was only when she was aboard the plane and she had switched her phone onto aeroplane mode that she allowed herself to think about what had happened. When she had left Crete 10 years earlier she had been a girl; now she was a young woman with a career making her way in the world in a different country. Exhausted, Popi slid in and out of sleep, but with nothing to divert her mind from her current situation she found it hard not to confront the reality of her father's death. Although she felt sad, her overwhelming state of mind was guilt at not feeling the full force of grief she thought she should be experiencing.

Her mind kept flitting to what she could remember of the island, the village and her old house, and she wondered if she would remember anyone. Beneath her the Alps looked spectacular, their snow-capped peaks gleaming in the morning sunlight. Going back to sleep, she awoke to the announcement that they were entering Greek air space and below was the island of Corfu. Looking out, Popi felt that the light had changed and with it something had lightened within her soul. As they began their descent the young woman marvelled at the small islands adrift on the bluest of seas, criss-crossed by the wakes of ferries, caiques and yachts. They flew over the caldera of Santorini, cruise ships moored in the crescent of the lagoon beneath the shimmering white of small villages perched precariously on the mountainside. The discomfort in Popi's ears signalled their approach to Heraklion, her first sight of the island when the aircraft banked before sweeping over beaches and dropping onto the cliff-top runway.

As the doors to the plane were flung open, the warmth of the spring day hit her and she felt the grief of something lost blowing in with the infusion of wild herbs: sage, thyme and rosemary. Her awareness heightened, Popi felt a mix of sorrow and comfort as she descended the stairs to board the bus to the terminal. The smells and sounds were redolent of a home she had not realised she missed.

Without thought, she fell back into her native tongue to ask where to pick up her car. Sitting in the driver's seat any sense of wellbeing she had felt on her arrival deserted her to be replaced by anxiety. Leaving the car park, vehicles seemed to come at her from all directions, drivers hooting their horns and shouting as they tried to assert their position on the road. As she nervously felt her way onto the national highway she tucked her car onto the right-hand side of the road, straddling the solid white line as traffic sped past.

Growing more familiar with the car she increased speed to match the restriction signs. Still she appeared to be the slowest vehicle on the road. Gradually she gained confidence but as her concentration returned to normal levels the space in her head taken up by anxiety about driving was replaced by thoughts of her dead father. Stepping onto the island brought back the memories she had blocked out for so many years.

Leaving the suburban sprawl of Heraklion behind, the road flirted with the coast. It skirted the sea before darting inland through the hills. Her route crossed bridges spanning dry valleys far below taking a road which had been blasted through the mountains. The traffic thinned as she passed signs indicating the resorts of Hersonissos and Malia before the road climbed steeply into the

Gorge of Selinari. Strong metal cages held back the rocks through which the highway had been carved, protecting motorists. Massive boulders frequently were dislodged from the hills by storms and the seismic activity which had given birth to the island and still grumbled and groaned somewhere deep beneath its surface.

Something stirred in her memory and she looked up. High above she spotted a pair of griffon vultures riding the thermals over the mountaintops. She recalled how she had come here as a girl with her parents and how they had told her that the vultures nest on the cliff faces of the canyon. As a child she had marvelled at these magnificent birds and dreamed of what it would be like to be free to fly so high above the mountains. How small she must have seemed to the creatures hovering thousands of feet above her, she thought. Somehow, these memories put her current misgivings into perspective, and made her feel more comfortable.

Chapter 3

MANOLIS PAUSED AND looked back at the parched piece of land on the waterfront. Stripped of its makeshift tarpaulin tents, boats, piles of wood, tools and other paraphernalia of his trade it looked much like the rest of the shoreline had before tourism had set a premium on land near the sea. He could not remember this spot without a boatyard upon it.

Some of his earliest memories were of his father working here and he could recall the stories his dad had told, fanciful or not, of the family business going back to Minoan times when their ancestors had chopped down cypress trees and dragged them down the mountainside with oxen to fashion the keels for the boats. Out of these grew vessels which traded olives between the bays on the north coast of the island.

He had always held in his mind the connection between himself and that ancient past where prior generations carved out the trunk of a single tree with bronze axes, steaming the curve of the prow and stern before chiselling out the mortise and tenon joints which fixed the side planks to the keel. The hull, covered in resin-treated linen painted with dolphins, fish and birds, would then be dragged into the water before fitting with its oars, mast of oak and square-rigged sail.

For as long ago as he could remember he had worked in the yard. He went to the local school and even to the *frontiesterio* to learn English, but he had always known his future lay in his father's business. His apprenticeship had been a formality as by the time he left school to take up his tools he was already a skilled craftsman.

Boatbuilding had taken an upturn. Ten years after the overthrow of the right-wing dictatorship, Greece was riding a wave of optimism under the progressive leadership of the charismatic Andreas Papandreou. His government had offered a 60 per cent subsidy for fishermen to build new boats. Many people still travelled around by sea and business was booming.

When he began working full-time, his father had trusted him enough to build a small boat for a local fisherman, only intervening when Manolis asked his advice. He had completed this build at the age of 16 and his first customer had been thrilled at the result. By the time his father's arthritis had made it impossible for him to carry on working, Manolis was a true master of his craft and more than capable of taking over the family business.

Now the seafront was empty, save for the shell of the half-built caique which had been his ruin. Silently Manolis shed a tear for what he had lost and wondered how the well of his happiness had been so easily drained. Katerina and Popi were in England, nearly 2,000 miles away. Manolis turned and walked towards the familiar comfort of the kafenio. But even here there was no escaping his memories. As he sat, Manolis recalled how it was in this very cafe that he had first met his wife all those years ago.

It had been a Sunday morning. Manolis loved the peace of the young day, before the sun was too hot and the water teased by the wakes of boats heading out to the island of Spinalonga. As usual on his day off, he had stopped for a coffee, to read the paper and watch the world go by. He was surprised to see a pretty young woman asking if she could pay her bill and inquiring of the waiter how best she could get to Spinalonga. Manolis still didn't remember what came over him that day, but the usually reserved boatbuilder stood up and crossed through the tables and chairs.

'I can take you, if you would like to go?' His smile immediately won the young woman over.

'I have a boat at my yard along the road and I'm not working today. I'm sorry, first let me introduce myself. My name is Manolis.'

'Katerina.' The smiling woman held out her hand. 'I would like that very much.'

His usual reticence gave way to a flood of questions as they left the square and took the coast road out of the village towards his yard. At first he bombarded Katerina with questions, so eager was he to discover as much as possible about her. She smiled at his enthusiasm but acquiesced, trying to fit in her answers before the next question was fired at her.

'Are you always this nosey when you meet a stranger?' she laughed.

'No. but I have never met a stranger like you before.'

'And I suppose you have never used that line before either?' Katerina blushed.

'I promise you no, I haven't. Should I shut up, am I saying too much? Please tell me about yourself and I will stop asking questions.'

As they walked, Katerina opened up to the handsome man she had only just met. There was something about him which made her relax into his company, his smile and easy manner coaxing her to talk about herself. She explained that she had just a week earlier arrived in Agios Nikolaos, where she had taken her first job at the hospital after qualifying as a nurse in Athens. She had never been to

Elounda before and had taken a taxi from the town on her day off in the hope of visiting the famous island of Spinalonga.

Manolis pointed out across the bay of Korfos to the fortified island which, for all the world, looked as though it was floating on a sea of glass.

'It was good you decided on an early start. If you had waited for the first bus, the island would already be busy with tourists. We will get there when the site opens at eight o'clock, before the crowds arrive on the big boats from Agios Nikolaos.'

'I decided to treat myself to a taxi as I didn't want to miss this beautiful part of the day.'

'You'd have missed me too!' Manolis was encouraged by the smile he got by way of reply.

Katerina couldn't help but feel she had been lucky to have met the young boatbuilder and suspected her smile may have given away as much.

Arriving at the ramshackle yard, Manolis pulled off his shirt and shoes and swam out to where his work boat was moored to a buoy fashioned from a plastic bottle anchored to the seabed. Pulling the cord on the outboard motor, as the engine sprung to life he brought the boat, bow first, onto the beach. Jumping out to retrieve his shirt and flip flops from the sand, he pulled himself back aboard before offering a hand to help Katerina climb up onto the deck.

Guiding her down into the cockpit of the boat, with Katerina seated on a thwart he reluctantly let go of her hand to take up the tiller, holding it central as he reversed away from the shore before swinging it over to set a course for Spinalonga. The small boat carved a path through the flat calm bay of Korfos, leaving a trail of white across the perfect blue of the sea. Even the chugging of the engine could not disturb the tranquillity of the early morning. Over the noise, Manolis found it hard to talk to the good-looking girl he had somehow managed to persuade to spend time with him. But her smile as she tilted her head back into the breeze created by the forward motion of the vessel reassured him. As her dark hair blew around her smiling face, she reached up to sweep it away from her striking dark brown eyes.

They approached the island and he manoeuvred the boat up to the small quay, leaving the helm to step forward and pass a rope through a mooring ring before helping Katerina ashore.

'I'll be back in a minute.' Manolis saw the momentary look of shock on her face as he jumped back aboard, untied the boat and reversed away.

'I'm just going to anchor so other boats can use the jetty,' he shouted.

Slinging the kedge overboard he dived into the water and swam back to the island.

'I'll soon dry off,' he said, laughing before remembering the crumpled notes in his pocket which he would need to pay the small entrance fee to the site.

'I've got money,' said a smiling Katerina.

Passing through Dante's Gate, the portal to the former leper colony, Katerina got an eerie sense of the island's past as Manolis explained that the patients that were exiled here knew they were unlikely ever to leave.

Although Katerina knew something of the island's history, the picture Manolis painted with his words enthralled her. He told her how the island had once been an impregnable Venetian fortress. Even after mainland Crete was ceded to the Turks in 1646, Spinalonga was only given up to the invaders following a treaty signed in 1715. The Turks in turn used it as a refuge when they felt under threat from Cretan nationalist uprisings. Then, just five years after the 1898 Four Powers agreement gave Crete its autonomy, the first peoples were sent into isolation there. It was not until 1957 that the final patients left the island, and a priest remained living there until 1962 to perform the rituals commemorating the last of the dead who were buried in the island's cemetery.

Beyond Dante's Gate, the 'Island of Tears' looked very much like any number of deserted Cretan villages. Flowers bloomed in the most impossible of places, forcing their way between cracks in the crumbling stones. Insects buzzed and a gecko scuttled across their path to find sanctuary beneath a boulder atop which a cat basked in the morning sunlight.

Despite the pain and isolation endured by the several hundred patients on the small island, Katerina found some of the personal stories Manolis told her life-affirming. The normality of day-to-day life was still held dear by the islanders. People fell in love and were married in the little church dedicated to Agios Panteleimonas, the patron saint of lepers, which had recently been restored on the main street. They had children and went about their lives in a way that was hard to imagine.

Leaving behind the tumbledown shops, tavernas and hospital, they skirted the island to the cliffs, where the remote cemetery looking seawards held those who had ended their days on Spinalonga. The compassionate young nurse shuddered, finding it hard to shake off this lingering reminder of their suffering. Sensing her discomfort, Manolis proffered a hand which Katerina gratefully took, leading her along the scrubby path which led beneath the old fortress back to the small quay.

Manolis dived into the clear blue water. Carefully navigating the armada of vessels starting to arrive at the island, he swam to his boat, hoisted himself aboard, fired the engine and went forward to weigh anchor. Awaiting his turn, he pulled the caique into the quay

44

and took Katerina's hand as she stepped aboard. Her smiling eyes met his as she thanked him but they couldn't help straying to the strong body to which his wet t-shirt clung.

'Have you plans for the rest of the day?' Manolis asked as he pulled the tiller towards him and they headed away from Spinalonga.

'The whole day is my own. I'm not at work again until tomorrow.' Katerina's face gave him the encouragement he needed to continue.

Manolis dropped the revs on the engine so they could hear each other more easily.

'Would you like to have lunch with me? It's a bit early, so we could go for a trip around the bay, then maybe a walk around Plaka before we eat. I can take you back to Agios Nikolaos later on my scooter, it's at the yard.'

'I'd love to,' she answered at once.

Manolis pushed the throttle forward, the engine getting louder. As they headed along the coast of the eastern peninsula of the bay, there was little need for words. Looking back at the striking fortress on the island, the pang of sorrow she felt at the plight of the former residents could not encroach for long on the happiness she was feeling.

She could not help but smile as she turned her gaze from the island to the man at the tiller, then across the water to the villages glinting white on the mountainsides covered with olive trees tumbling down into the bay. Tourist boats heading from harbour identified the strip of buildings along the coastline as Elounda, where just a few hours before fate had brought her together with Manolis. What that fate held in store for her she did not know, but for the moment she was content just to let life take its course.

Passing through the narrow canal under the bridge linking the peninsula with the mainland, they anchored above what Manolis told her was the ancient city of Olous. Katerina would have loved to dive down to the seabed, but she had not packed a swimming costume. Maybe, if there were to be a next time…

As they talked, they relaxed into each other's company. Returning through the channel, Manolis skirted the western shore, periodically dropping the boat's speed so he could point out landmarks as they went, the sail-less windmills, submerged salt pans, a disused warehouse and what had been a carob factory. Holidaymakers were already staking claim to the sunbeds and umbrellas dotting the small strips of sand on the shoreline. A sailboard skimmed across the rippling water and the young nurse felt the cooling spray blown up by the rising breeze. As the wind increased and Manolis headed the boat into the oncoming waves, Katerina screamed and laughed, tickled by the cold water. He grinned.

By the time they reached Plaka, they needed a walk to dry off in the now baking sun before lunch. They strolled alongside the seafront tavernas before browsing the shops displaying pottery, clothes and all sorts of woven goods. Then they returned to the waterfront, taking a taverna table a few feet above the bay looking across to Spinalonga. Neither of them would forget that first meal together. Both were hungry from the sea air and early start, so they tucked into a shared platter of fish. Crunchy fried calamari, huge pink prawns in oil, rich octopus, charred sardines and glittering sea bass with salad and bread were perfectly accompanied by a chilled wine, droplets of condensation running down the cold glass carafe.

That was just the start of the happy times. From that moment they both knew they should be together and it was only a matter of months before Manolis proposed. It was less than a year from the day they met that they married in the church in the village looking down on the bay. Their course was set fair for a happy marriage and when the couple discovered that they were to have a baby they both nearly overflowed with joy.

If Manolis had secretly longed for a boy, he did not show it and Katerina marvelled at the way he bonded with the little girl. When she returned to work at the hospital, Popi would spend some of the day with Manolis' parents but often would be found asleep in a cot he had fashioned out of off-cuts in the shade of the tarpaulin in his yard. Five years later, after they lost Manolis' father and shortly afterwards his mother, the young girl would be dropped off in the morning at school by her father and go to his yard yard when lessons were over.

Although Manolis had never admitted it to himself, when his daughter was born, he had subconsciously hoped for a son who would follow in his footsteps. In the years that followed he and his wife had tried for another child, but it was not to be. He doted on his daughter, however, and she showed an affinity to the sea. As she grew, her interest in his work made him hope that maybe she could keep the business running when he retired.

At the end of a school day, Popi would run down the hill and along the coast road to her father's yard hoping that he could find her a job to do. If not, she would watch him at work, storing away somewhere in her memory the skills he showed her. Sometimes she would be tasked with scrubbing off the bottom of the hulls of boats dragged up on the foreshore before applying a new coat of paint in readiness for the coming season. When such jobs were finished, she would take a swim whilst waiting for her father to complete whatever job he was doing. Then father and daughter would board the small caique and head out into the bay. From a young age, Manolis had let his daughter take the tiller. Some days they would head past the island of Spinalonga and others through the canal and into the bay of Mirabello. They would even go out in winter or when the sea was rough, sticking within the shelter of the bay of Korfos. Manolis taught his daughter how to head into the oncoming waves or run with the sea astern, and how to anchor in the lee of a bay to ride out a storm. Around the boat she was sure-footed, strong and calm and he was proud of his daughter's prowess.

'It's in your blood Popi,' he would tell her, frequently regaling her with the stories his father had told him about the unbroken thread which linked them to the Minoans.

Distraught at what he had lost, despite the early hour Manolis ordered raki and regaled anyone who would listen with the history of his demise. Although many of his friends had heard the story before they listened to him in sympathy, not wanting to leave the distressed man alone with his thoughts and the drink.

The year Manolis and Katerina married, the seeds of disaster were sown but the couple were too caught up in their happiness to see the warning signs. In 1996 an EU directive ushered in a law offering fishermen vast compensation payments to destroy their boats in an attempt to control over-fishing. In the years that followed more than two thirds of Greece's fishing fleet had been bulldozed. This directive was the beginning of the end for most traditional boatbuilders in the country. Not only were orders for new craft almost unheard of, but demand for maintenance work was also shrinking with the fleet.

The world economic crash of 2007 followed by the Greek debt crisis and austerity measures imposed by the troika plunged the business even deeper into financial trouble. Katerina was having to work many extra hours unpaid at the hospital as health services were stretched to breaking point, and until the end of the month she was never sure if she would be paid at all. Short of capital, the banks were unwilling to extend any credit and were brutal in collecting debts. To top this off, local government used all means possible to usurp a business if it could make more money from businesses set up to serve the tourist trade, which they saw as their economic saviour.

It was in this perfect storm that Manolis and Katerina's marriage had struggled to stay afloat. But Manolis had been thrown a lifeline in the form of a commission to build a caique. Desperate to secure the job, he agreed a small upfront deposit and borrowed heavily from private sources to fund the initial work on the build. When the customer pulled out of the deal Manolis was left high and dry with nowhere to go. Unable to pay his rent on the shorefront land, his business was closed down by the authorities.

Exhausted, stressed and broke, the couple had been unable to see their way through the crisis. All Katerina could think about was the lack of any future their life offered for Popi, and the more her husband retreated into the temporary comforts of the kafenio, the more her anger grew. Their rows got worse and the more they expressed their frustration at each other, the more they hated themselves.

Manolis could see nowhere to turn. He had no other skills, and anyway no jobs were available anywhere. Katerina had seen nursing positions available in the UK at wages beyond her wildest dreams. With her marriage on the verge of collapse, she saw no other way to secure a future for her daughter.

They both cried when Katerina said that she was leaving. The tears were for what they had lost somewhere along the way. In spite of his regret, Manolis had no more fight. Part of him knew that his wife was right and there was no future for their child in Greece. He had let both his wife and daughter down. He could not even look after himself, let alone his family. As he sat and drank, the raki momentarily took the edge off his despair, and if it later was to kill him, what had he to live for?

It was early evening as the two men sat sharing a carafaki of raki. Manolis' brother-in-law had been alerted by a friend returning to the village that his help and support might be needed to see him home.

'*Yamas*, Manoli! We should leave after this one. Come home with me and Thea will prepare us a meal.'

Spyros stood to help his brother-in-law up from his chair. While Manolis struggled to stand, a man as overdressed for the heat as he was overweight pushed through the door to the kafenio.

'What's that heap of junk doing on my land?' said the new arrival.

It took a few seconds before the Manolis recognised him; then followed a moment of clarity. Launching himself, he grabbed the gold medallion which hung round the man's neck.

'You bastard!'

Spyros seized Manolis by both arms and pulled him back. He could only just hold the strong boatbuilder; had he not been so drunk he would not have been able to restrain him.

A bead of sweat ran down the fat man's face. Sensing he may have misjudged the situation he backed away to the door, stopping to reach for a handkerchief to dab at the perspiration. Slightly less confident now, he left his parting words hanging in the air.

'I want that boat off my land. My builders move in next week.'

Spyros held on to Manolis for a moment but he felt the fight draining out of him to be replaced by despair.

'Another raki,' Spyros shouted to the taverna owner. 'Thea won't mind if we're a bit late for our supper.'

Slumped in his chair, the appearance of Christos had brought a sobering lucidity to Manolis.

'That was Christos, the businessman who commissioned the boat. The bastard set me up to get further in debt so that I would be thrown off the land and he could buy the lease.

I so wanted and needed the work that I let him get away with a paltry deposit whilst I bought all the materials to get the job underway. He tipped me over the edge and he knew exactly what he was doing.'

All Spyros could do was listen to his brother-in-law as his anger turned to resignation. If he had been at rock bottom moments before, now he was being held there by the weight of the realisation of how the businessman had manipulated him to cheat him out of his boatyard.

It was after midnight before Spyros managed to get Manolis back to his house. He was past eating anything as he was helped into the spare bedroom and Thea covered her brother up and got water for the bedside table. To the sound of snoring echoing through the walls Spyros told his wife what he had discovered.

The next morning, as Manolis came to, he was hit by the full potency of his hangover and the truth of what had happened the previous evening. Letting himself out the door, he returned to his own house and from the shed took a can of petrol and some rags. He would get rid of that 'heap of junk' on the waterfront. It had done nothing but brought him to ruin. Lost him his wife and daughter, destroyed his livelihood and his self-respect.

It took him longer than usual to walk down the donkey path to the sea. The early morning sun hurt his eyes, his throat was parched and his body ached. He skirted past the cafes and shops on the edge of town, ashamed to be seen and furtive about what he was about to do.

Standing on the shoreline which had once been his yard he looked out over the bay towards Spinalonga. He remembered the first day he had met Katerina and how she had been moved by the resilience of the people who had once lived their lives there. But they had no choice, just as he had no choice now. He turned and walked towards the frame of the caique chocked up on the beach and held upright by props. It was splendid, every curve in the timber he had steamed, every joint he had cut by hand. He ran a finger across the wood which he had so lovingly sanded. He turned away with a tear in his eye and took the lid off the can.

As he lifted the petrol to soak a rag, Manolis noticed two vehicles approaching along the coast road. Better wait until they passed. Through his befuddled mind he recognised Spyros' four-wheel drive pulling a trailer turning onto the beach, then Yiannis from the garage getting out of his flat-bed truck accompanied by his two apprentices.

'We thought we'd come to give you a hand.' Spyros swept his hair out of his eyes as he approached Manolis followed by the other three men.

Reaching for the can he took it from his brother-in-law, replacing the cap. 'You don't want to do that. We can take the boat to your house. It has some worth and you never know, you may be able to finish it some day.'

Manolis hesitated. Hadn't he wanted to rid himself of any reminder of his past life, the pain of losing everyone and everything that was dear to him?. He reached to take the can back from Spyros.

'Do you really want to forget everything about the past? The wonderful times you had with your wife and daughter, the wonderful boats you and your family have crafted for centuries. Don't destroy the boat. Keep it until you are thinking straight. If over time you think it's the right decision you can do it later. Trust me, Manoli.'

'And how do you propose we get it up the mountain?' Manolis shrugged.

'On my boat trailer.'

'I can see that, but how do we get it on the trailer.' As he said it Manolis could see the two apprentices lifting an engine hoist from the back of Yiannis' truck.

'I suppose it isn't that heavy without any planking, decks or fittings. If we hoist the bow onto the roller on the trailer, then lift up the stern and use the trailer winch to move it into position, we could do it.'

Despite his reservations about not destroying the boat, Manolis found himself caught up in the challenge of getting it onto the trailer. Usually, after a hull had been fashioned it would be winched down to the sea over rollers on the beach and fitted out there. If it needed to be taken out of the sea it would be put on a trailer on a slipway and dragged out or hoisted out by crane.

Manolis scrambled to the top of the craft and nailed two struts of wood between the opposite gunwales to keep it rigid. Working methodically the men managed to get the boat in position before the trailer winch wound it forwards onto the cradle supports. Ropes were brought from Spyros' truck to secure the skeleton to the trailer. Within a couple of hours, the convoy made its way slowly off the beach onto the coast road.

They squeezed their way through the narrow streets of Elounda, Yiannis driving in front to clear a path for the large load. As they got onto the mountain road any traffic coming towards them, instead of hooting their horns with impatience, pulled over or backed up the mountain. Word had got out about what had happened the night before in the taverna, and some even clapped as the procession slowly snaked its way up the hillside.

The load was too wide to get through the village lanes, so they headed above the houses to where Manolis' small olive grove bordered the road. The men laboured to dismantle a section of the dry-stone walling wide enough for truck and trailer to pass through before reversing it in among the trees. The chocks and props were unloaded and the boat carefully winched backwards into position.

Manolis thanked his friends for their help. He was uncertain how he felt about having the boat there as a constant reminder of what he had lost. But for the first time in some months, he felt he had achieved something.

Chapter 4

DESPITE ALL THAT had happened during the day, Popi knew she wouldn't sleep and changed her mind and poured another measure of Metaxa into her glass. Her uncle and aunt were now sleeping upstairs and all was quiet. Popi sat out on the terrace of the village house which had been her childhood home and had now been bequeathed to her. She had been back in Crete for fewer than two days and already felt a sense of belonging.

Cradling her drink, she sat mesmerised by the lights of Elounda flickering at the bottom of the mountainside. The faint sound of a puttering engine drew her attention to the navigation lights of a small fishing boat passing through the channel into the bay. The lights were still on at the smart taverna which now stood beside the canal as late diners lingered over their meals. Popi's mind wandered back to the happy times she had spent out on the water with her father when she had snorkelled over the ruins of the lost city of Olous.

As she floated, swam and dived she had been transported back to when this was a Minoan port inhabited by thousands of people making a living trading whetstones, olives and dye from seashells with other cities on the island.

On calm days, the stone foundations of the city and its streets could clearly be made out on the seabed; the sunken city some believed a result of the same cataclysmic seismic upheaval which had devastated the island of Santorini in the second millennium BCE. Others thought the city's demise to be more recent, the land being tilted beneath the waves by an earthquake of 780 AD.

Drifting in that watery silence Popi could imagine the citizens going about their business and her mind would wander to the great city of Knossos which she had visited with her parents on the outskirts of Heraklion. Did the boats made by her ancestors brave the seas and travel west along the coast from here to supply the court of the great King Minos?

Where the smart taverna now stood, sometimes she and her father would step ashore and stroll behind the rickety bar that then stood there on the peninsula to see the Byzantine mosaic, sole remains of an early Christian basilica, its vibrant leaping dolphins and fish exposed for anyone passing to enjoy. In the shade of the dusty churchyard of the chapel of Anilipsi they would stare out to sea imagining what it must have been like before the canal was dug out by French sailors in the twilight years of the 19th century. Before that time, seafarers caught in a storm in the bay of Mirabello would have to brave the seas around the headland of Kalidon before finding sanctuary in the lagoon of Korfos through the straits of Spinalonga.

Popi thought back to her father's yard on the beach where a taverna now sat, hidden from her view by the hillside of olive groves. Despite the darkness a cockerel crowed, waking a sleeping dog from its slumbers, prompting a round of barking to echo around the hills.

After arriving in England, her mother had encouraged her not to look back, determined that Popi should make a future for herself in her adopted homeland. But sitting here in the village in which she had been born, Popi felt inexorably drawn to reminiscing about her childhood. She knew that her mother had only been trying to protect her from the agonies of the breakdown of her marriage, but now her feelings were confused and a tear ran down her cheek at the thought of a past which might have been.

Although her mother had never criticised her father, she had not encouraged talk of him or the past. It was only in that moment today when she looked down on Turtle Beach that she realised how she had suppressed her desire to see her father again. The memories, condolences and kind wishes of his friends at the funeral had convinced Popi that her father had been a good and well-loved man. What had Spyros called him? 'The best of men.' She loved and respected her uncle and trusted his judgement. Even Costas, her father's former apprentice, had taken the trouble to travel from Agios Nikolaos that evening to pay his respects.

Whether it was the brandy or the funeral, the events of the day began to catch up with Popi and she felt her mood shift towards maudlin. She had to drag herself back before she sank into the depression which sometimes pulled her down. She tried to turn her thoughts to her mother back in England and how she had spent her life doing what she believed was best for her only daughter. Out of nowhere, Popi remembered that first night in England when her mother had cuddled her, comforting her until she slept. She realised how much she owed her. That night and every day since, her mother had been there for Popi and had helped her weather the storm.

She recalled how the following morning the rain had stopped as they opened the door to step out onto the streets of Salisbury. The sun peeped through the clouds scudding past the cathedral spire, the breeze bringing with it the scent of a fresh new day. In their own ways both mother and daughter had come to an unconscious decision, not to look back.

On that first day, Katerina wanted find out where the hospital was so she would not get lost when she began her induction the following week. Then she would take Popi for lunch before they went to meet the head teacher at the new school she would be starting at in a couple of days.

If Katerina was reassured by her first impressions of what was to be her new place of work, Popi was more daunted by the large comprehensive - both the size of the building and the number of students quite different from the local school she had attended in Crete. The head teacher appeared kind and put Popi at ease when she complimented her on her English. She introduced her to a fellow pupil who had been assigned to be her mentor and took Popi to the store to get a second-hand uniform whilst the head teacher reassured her mother that she would be well looked after. Leaving the school that day, although still nervous of what lay in store, both mother and daughter felt happier about living in a new country.

From that day Popi realised that her mother had devoted her life to ensuring she had a secure future. Although she must have been afraid of what that future might bring, Katerina had worked hard to successfully rebuild their lives. Thinking of her mother's new-found happiness with Andrew made Popi smile and she hauled on the lifeline of that thought to drag herself out of her sorrow. Picking up her drink, she walked down the steps from the terrace and around the side of the house. There, beneath the trees was the shell of the caique her father had so lovingly built. She felt a thrill at the long grass on her legs, and the leaves of the olive trees rustling in the breeze.

Popi approached the boat slowly; there was something about it that demanded reverence. She held out her hand and ran it along the keel, stringers and strakes. Even in the dark she could sense the beauty of the caique and the love which had been put into its crafting. Looking through the silhouette in the moonlight, with the grasses and wildflowers of the olive grove brushing against the sturdy keel, the embryonic boat looked as though it had grown out of this earth. But, seeing its size, Popi was aware of the effort it must have taken to get the vessel up here from the coast.

She sat down on the grass and let her mind wander. Her uncle had said that all this would be hers. She already sensed a connection she had not felt in England. She was truly at home here and the bones of the caique gave her a tangible link to her dead father.

Popi closed her eyes as tiredness caught up with her. She stood up, finished her drink and then, setting her glass down on the terrace table, she made her way to her bedroom. Sleep came easily, her slumbers untroubled.

Despite only a few hours' sleep, she awoke as the first vestiges of the new day crept into her room through the cracks in the old blue shutters. Feeling strangely refreshed, she could hear the table being set for breakfast on the terrace. She pulled back the wooden slide bolt of the window and opened the shutters to see her aunt busying herself below.

'*Kalimera*, Thea. How are you this morning?' Her aunt looked up, smiling.

'I'm good; it is going to be a lovely day. Did you sleep well?'

'Better than I deserve to, I think. Give me a moment and I'll be down to help you.'

'*Siga, siga*, slowly, slowly. Take your time, we are in no rush. I'm happy to do this.'

Dressing and coming downstairs, Popi found Spyros in the kitchen laying out plates of meat, cheese and hard-boiled eggs, yoghurt and honey.

'And here's some fresh bread and croissants from the bakery,' he said. 'I took a walk down to Elounda this morning. It is going to be a hot day for so early in the year I think.' Her uncle picked up a laden tray and carried it out to the terrace.

'I'll make some coffee,' Popi offered.

'All done.' Spyros looked back over his shoulder. 'Come outside and relax.'

In the morning sunlight Popi took in the display of geraniums growing in the containers - violet and pink. A scarlet bougainvillea clung to the side of the house, and looking up she saw a vine

64

creeping across the pergola. Sitting at the wooden table, she remembered how her father had crafted it from off-cuts of wood when she was a child. A canopy of olive trees drifted down the mountainside, dotted with the deep red of spring poppies which burst from the brown earth beneath. In the distance the bay of Korfos gleamed invitingly as Popi spooned some yoghurt into a bowl, scattered some nuts on top and drizzled them with honey.

As they sat over breakfast a question came from Popi's lips before she realised it had even formed in her mind.

'Would it take much to finish the caique?'

Spyros put his small coffee cup back on its saucer and smiled at his wife.

'We have some of the wood from your father's yard stored in our outbuilding. It would need an engine as the one your father bought was repossessed. More wood, fittings, paint and so on. Perhaps thirty thousand euros would do it, but I'm no expert. The real problem would be finding a boatbuilder capable of doing the skilled work.'

Undeterred, Popi outlined a plan that had formed unconsciously, it seemed, while she slept. She explained how she would like to finish the boat to honour the memory of her father and to continue her family's link to the sea. Without knowing where the idea had come from, she talked about starting ecological boat cruises by day, maybe diving and snorkelling and sunset barbecue trips in the evenings where she could explain to guests the wonders of the night sky and how the stars related to Greek myths and legends. She loved the sea, after all she was a marine biologist, a skill that maybe could find her a niche in the tourist market. None of these ideas had been thought out or costed. But the more she spoke, the more they seemed like a good idea.

'That all sounds brilliant. So you think you might stay on here?' Smiling, her uncle raised a questioning eyebrow.

In forming plans to get the boat finished and what she would do with it, her sleeping mind had not addressed such practicalities as leaving her mother behind in England and giving up a job she had worked so hard to secure, let alone where she would find the money to fund the project. Her uncle's question brought her down to earth with a bump.

Spyros could see his remark had deflated the young woman.

'Of course it can be done, and I will help you all I can. But you need to think long and hard to be sure it is what you want. Life here in Crete is still difficult. But if you are determined, I'm sure you will find a way to follow your dream.'

Popi smiled. At the moment it was just an idea which had formed in her sleep, and the irony of her uncle's words had not passed her by.

'Have you plans for the day?' she asked her aunt and uncle. 'Do you still have your boat?'

'Of course we have the boat. We are going to move back to our own house if you think you will be OK on your own. Other than that we are free. Why do you ask?

'I would love to get out on the water. Would you have time to take me, uncle?'

'I'd love to. We'll just get home and make up a picnic, perhaps we can do a spot of fishing and if you want I can bring some snorkels? Give us an hour and I'll pick you up in the truck from outside the church.'

'I'd love that. Don't worry about the breakfast things, I'll clear away.' Popi rose and began to stack the plates.

*

Spyros' boat was dazzling. It stood out from the workaday vessels rubbing alongside it moored up to the harbour wall in Elounda. White and blue, a painted eye to ward off evil spirits stared out from each side of its sparkling bow. Named after Thea, its topsides reflected the rays of the midday sun in its gleaming varnish.

The boat was cherished by Spyros. It had been built by Manolis in the days when Spyros' burgeoning architecture business was just taking off, and Spyros knew that the boatbuilder who would soon be his brother-in-law had given it to him for less than it had cost to make it. Since the demise of Manolis' yard, every year in autumn Spyros would haul the boat out on his trailer at the slipway and through the winter refresh all the paintwork and service the engine before returning it to the waters of the bay around the following Easter.

Spyros jumped onto the foredeck, going aft to loosen the stern line before returning to the bow to pull the boat nearer the shore. He held out a hand to Thea, who stepped aboard. Before he could offer assistance to Popi she had bridged the gap and already stood at the prow. Whilst Spyros started the engine, his wife stowed the food and drinks below in the cool box and Popi cast off the bow lines. Spyros eased the boat astern then engaged forward gear, swinging the helm over and steering a long arc out past the taverna on the harbour wall and into the bay.

As Popi moved to the cockpit, her uncle nodded and she confidently took the tiller, pushing the throttle forward as they reached open water setting a course behind a boat ferrying tourists to Spinalonga. As they increased speed the boat settled into a comfortable pitch, throwing up a slight spray which dried almost instantly on the hot decks. The blue and white flag of Greece strained at its halyard. Popi could not think of a flag which could more perfectly represent the colours of the sea and sky. The coast ahead was deserted, but looking back on Elounda and along the peninsula to the canal they could see dots of brightly-coloured beachwear, umbrellas and inflatable toys like an impressionist painting as early-season holidaymakers enjoyed the sands.

Spyros pointed landwards and Popi responded by dropping the speed and heading into a small deserted bay. Looking down, she could see through the gin-clear water all the way to the sea bed. Going forward, her uncle threw out the anchor. Popi let the boat drift backwards, taking up the slack in the chain before cutting the engine. In contrast to the beaches on the other side of the bay, here it was deserted. The only thing to ruffle the still waters of the cove was the occasional wash of a distant boat.

Beneath the moored caique, Popi made out an octopus scuttling to and from its garden of pebbles and shells at the edge of some rocks. Shoals of fish flitted in and out of the seaweed floating near the shoreline. She could not resist the allure of the water and went below to change into her swimming costume. Not even the sight of a sea snake raising its head above the water as it whipped across the surface could stop her from grabbing a mask, snorkel and fins and diving in.

The water was cold but refreshing after the heat of the sun beating on the deck of the boat. After diving down and exploring the sea bed, Popi lay on her back and let the salty water buoy her up. She closed her eyes. It felt as if she was the only person floating in this watery world. That moment felt so perfect that she wanted to hold onto it forever. Adrift in the comforting amniotic fluid of the bay she was reminded of her childhood days swimming in these very waters. Would it be possible for her to forge a plan that would enable her dream to become a reality?

Her life in England was comfortable enough. For years she had known no different but somehow, back on Crete, she felt as though she fitted in, that she had a place in the world. Silently floating in the tranquil water of the cove cleared her mind and she started to focus on what her future might hold.

Having her father's old house in the village, there would be no rent to pay, and the income from the olive grove, if she lived frugally would perhaps be enough to keep body and soul together. Although she and her mother would miss each other if she stayed, Katerina had found happiness with Andrew. Both women were now finding their own way in a new chapter of their lives.

'Don't float for too long - you will burn!' Popi was shaken from her musing by Spyros' shout.

'Come back and we'll have something to eat.'

Her uncle hung a rope ladder over the side and Popi climbed aboard. Seeing the feast Thea had put out on the cockpit table she realised how hungry she was. Salads, cheese and spinach pies, vine leaves stuffed with rice, tzatziki and bread. Large plastic bottles of red wine and water were also unearthed from the chiller.

'Help yourselves.' Thea placed plates in front of Popi and her husband.

She did not have to be asked twice. The snorkelling had left Popi famished. Looking around her at the bay and at her kindly aunt and uncle she pondered the event which had brought her here. Her father's death had made her sad, but for so long she hadn't known him. She felt a tinge of guilt at the happiness she now felt about her present situation. If only she could get together the wherewithal to be able to finish the boat perhaps she could both stay and honour the memory of her father.

Replete, they stashed the empty plates below and Spyros rigged an awning over the boom to keep off the afternoon sunshine. Refilling their glasses, the three of them sat with their own thoughts as the boat slowly danced around the anchor warp in the afternoon breeze.

'Whilst you were in the water, Thea and I were talking. About what you said earlier. About your father's caique.'

Popi opened her eyes, pulling herself forward on the bench seat as her uncle spoke.

'I am not a rich man, but my business has been doing quite well recently. When I first started out, your father gave me a lot of help

71

and support. This boat, I know he did not charge me anything like what he should have for the work he did on it. More recently he sometimes helped me out if a carpenter let me down, and despite his hardships would not accept payment. I would like to make you an offer. I will give you the money to finish the boat, if you will let me become your business partner? You can repay me your share of the money when the business is up and running but we can discuss the details later.'

Popi's face gave the answer her uncle wanted even before she could blurt out, 'Thank you, that is really kind of you, uncle.'

'To our future business. *Yamas*, cheers.'

Immediately Popi's head was brimming with plans. She told her uncle her ideas to call the daytime boat trips Underwater Safaris and the evening sailings 'Stars and Legends'.

Spyros smiled at his niece's enthusiasm. 'We need to find someone who can finish the boat first. Leave it with me and I will make some enquiries.'

'Perhaps one of the first things you should do is to talk it through with your mother.' Thea interrupted.

'I don't want her to think that the first time you step foot back on the island, we abduct you by persuading you to stay. Then you will need to think about resigning from your job, and if you are sure that you want to give up your academic career.'

The practicalities of taking on this new venture for a moment punctured the bubble of optimism that Popi had been feeling. Seeing her face fall, Thea reassured her. 'I'm sure your mum will be fine with it, just take some time to think things over before you commit to such a huge change in your life.'

Thea was right; this was a life-changing decision. Sitting on her uncle's boat in a small cove surrounded by the imposing mountains staring across the bay towards Spinalonga, Popi had never been more sure of anything in her life.

As the afternoon wore on, the heat of the sun abated and Spyros reached into a locker, pulling out two fishing lines. Starting the engine, he navigated the boat over the anchor as Popi operated the winch to bring it aboard. A line of spinners was set out astern to starboard and Spyros baited up the hooks on the other and cast it out to port as he moved the boat forwards into the bay. Throwing a bucket attached to a rope overboard, he filled it with water.

'Now let's see if we can catch our supper.'

Sitting up on the foredeck, Popi soaked up the late afternoon sun as her uncle steered the boat south towards the canal. She longed to go to Turtle Beach but remembered her promise to her father to keep it secret.

With the mast up they were unable to pass under the bridge and Spyros was content to turn his boat northwards towards Spinalonga.

As the sun dropped lower in the sky, the honey-coloured stone of the buildings on the island glowed with a warmth which belied its recent history. The last of the tour boats were leaving for the day as Spyros put the engine in neutral and hauled in the spinners. Nothing had taken the lures. Stowing it back in the locker he reached for the baited trolling line. As soon as he felt the weight he knew they had been lucky. The hooks were alive with a lustrous catch of sardines. Popi helped her uncle disgorge fish from the hooks and put them in the bucket.

Back at their house in the village, Spyros wasted no time in piling the charcoal into the half oil drum he had fashioned into a barbecue. Whilst waiting for it to glow he gutted the fish, slashing their silver skins with a knife before liberally coating them with salt. Thea sat at the outside table chopping tomatoes, onions and cucumber before adding a slab of crumbly white feta to the salad.

Popi lit the lanterns and lifted them onto the wall. The sound of a lone goat bell accompanied the last cicada song as the candles cast their long shadows onto the terrace. Popi, Thea and Spyros sat down together to eat. Through the waves of olive trees spilling down the hillside, they could make out the bay now transformed from ultramarine to black. Above them the stars shone with a brightness that had been unimaginable to Popi in England and yet she easily pointed out the different constellations to her aunt and uncle, weaving tales of Greek myths and legends, stories of the Trojan wars and Homer's *Odyssey* inspired by the night sky. Her aunt and uncle were spellbound and by the time she had finished, they were convinced that her idea of evening boat tours providing a similar experience to tourists would be a success.

Later, as Popi made her way up the hill through the narrow village lanes to her father's house she was filled with excitement about the new venture. If Spyros could find a boatbuilder to finish the caique, she was sure she could make a go of things. She was nervous about taking this new course in her life, but in her heart she knew she was making the right choice.

Popi looked at her watch. It was already 2.15 in the morning. She considered phoning her mother but decided that even with the two-hour time difference that she would be in bed if she was not working nights. The following day was a Saturday, so with a bit of luck her mother would not be at the hospital. She would try to phone the next day.

Although late to bed, Popi had difficulty sleeping. She kept going over and over in her head what she would say to her mum. Swept up on the wave of enthusiasm for the project, she had convinced herself that her mother wouldn't mind. Now she had Andrew she had got a new life, and anyway Crete was not that far away, was it? What had seemed so certain in the light of day, in the darkness before the dawn seemed to yank at her insecurities. Her mother had sacrificed so much to secure her a good future and Popi had worked hard to get her degree and find a job at the university.

Getting up early, she opened the shutters and the clean bright light of the morning went some way towards banishing her negative thoughts. She made herself a traditional Greek coffee in a briki on the hob and took it out to the table on the terrace. It was much too early to phone her mum and the waiting allowed the uncertainties she felt about the impending conversation creep back in. She knew her mother would be up and about by 8 o'clock, which meant she would need to wait until 10 to phone her.

Popi walked down the terrace steps to the olive grove which surrounded the house. The bay below was like a polished mirror glinting in a frame of gnarled olive trees. Rounding the side of the house she caught her first glimpse of the caique in daylight. If at night it had an ethereal quality, in the early morning sunlight it revealed its true splendour, a commanding presence setting sail on a sea of mountains.

From its frame, Popi could envisage how magnificent the finished vessel would look. Every piece of wood was in perfect proportion, all fitting snugly together and displaying the elegant curves which would grace the boat when it was finished. Seeing it she could understand how her father had kept it that long. The boat was more than just a few pieces of timber joined together. It was as though it was a living thing, created with skills which went back all the way to when the first Europeans lived in these parts. It was a link which connected Popi to the past, making her feel happy.

She stepped over the keel and through the skeleton, surveying each joint and looking for any sign of rot or infestation on the unprotected wood. The timber had weathered well and, if anything, any discolouring added to its natural beauty. When finished and coated in a depth of varnish the stains, grain and knots would display the story of the caique's crafting. If Popi had been wavering about finishing the boat, she was now more determined than ever to follow her dream. It gave her the resolve she needed to phone her mother.

Katerina was pleased to get her call that Saturday morning. When Popi got to the real point of the conversation, her mum sounded enthusiastic and cheery. She said that her business plans sounded exciting; that she had always liked and trusted Spyros and that his offer to pay to finish the boat was kind. When Popi asked how she was, her mother said that she was going on a picnic with Andrew out on Salisbury Plain, but that it had just started raining so perhaps they would go for a pub lunch instead.

Ending the call, Popi began to breathe more normally. She walked down the lane towards her aunt and uncle's house, determined to let them know the good news. She didn't know why she had been worried about calling her mum. Katerina had always been supportive of her in everything she wanted to do. That her mother and Andrew were so happy together further reassured Popi that she need not worry about her mum as she waved to her aunt and uncle who were still sitting outside eating breakfast.

Chapter 5

AS SHE REPLACED the receiver, Katerina took a deep breath and a tear escaped from one eye, cutting a cold course down her cheek.

She was delighted to hear her daughter happy, but had immediately sensed the breathless Popi had some news to tell her. As they went through the pleasantries, chatted about the funeral and about Thea and Spyros, Katerina was already composing herself for the surprise she suspected was coming. She hoped she had sufficiently disguised her anxieties about her daughter returning to live in Crete, giving up a good job and being so far away from her in England.

'Are you alright?' Andrew came into the room, the big man wrapping his arms around his girlfriend.

'I'm fine, just being a bit silly that's all,' sniffed Katerina, searching for a tissue.

It came as a shock to hear her daughter's plans to stay in Crete, but not entirely a surprise. Deep in her soul she too felt the pull of her homeland, although with the death of her former husband she had little to connect her with the island.

She had no surviving family. During the years of the far-right Junta her father, a journalist, had been imprisoned in exile. He died shortly after his liberation in 1974, his health ruined by the torture, starvation and sleep deprivation meted out by that barbaric regime. Her mother followed him to the grave, dying of a broken heart, so the young Katerina was told. An only child, she had been brought up by her grandparents who had long since died while she was a young student in Athens.

Despite that, Katerina could not escape the inexplicable longing for home which crept up on her in moments of solitude. Sometimes she saw the same in her daughter's eyes, as though only returning to Crete would make her whole.

In her heart Katerina was pleased for her daughter; if she could find a way to survive in Crete, she would support her. She had heard in Popi's voice the happiness and excitement she felt. She knew her tears were selfish. She had her own new life with Andrew now and recognised she must cut the cord that bound her to her daughter and let her lead her own life.

She let her head relax into Andrew's chest. How lucky she was to have found him. He took the tissue from her hand and dabbed her eyes dry.

'Let's get off for lunch and you can tell me about it,' he said.

*

Thea was pleased when Popi told them how well Katerina had taken the news. She smiled as her husband and Popi excitedly discussed ideas, but somewhere inside she knew that her former sister-in-law would be hurting. Although enthusiastic, Spyros realised that if Popi was to turn her dream to reality they would need to make a firm business plan. He brought his laptop onto the terrace and began making a list of actions for them both. Firstly, they needed to set up the business and a bank account. Spyros suggested that they visit his solicitor and accountant in Agios Nikolaos, both of whom would be able to help Popi sort out her father's estate as well as draw up the necessary paperwork for their new joint venture.

Spyros promised to phone to make the appointments, and early on Tuesday the new business partners headed for Agios Nikolaos. The forms seemed endless and Spyros could sense Popi's frustration at the remorseless bureaucracy involved. Well versed in the sometimes seemingly impenetrable maze of the system, Spyros reassured his niece that things would get done eventually and that all that was required was patience. When they had done everything they could for the day, Spyros suggested that they go for lunch, leaving things in the hands of the professionals.

Popi had not been to the heart of the town since she was a child but as they walked down a flight of steps the memory of the alluring sunken lake flooded her senses. It had not changed. Beneath a sheer cliff, small fishing boats drifted at their moorings on the glistening bottomless lake. Popi remembered her father had told her that the goddess Athena and her sister Artemis had bathed in the fathomless waters. Tavernas and cafes perched on the water's edge. A tiny whitewashed chapel hewn from the vertical rock, a single bell hanging from its arched belfry, was the irresistible subject of many photographs snapped here.

A tiny caique made its way through the cutting, under the narrow bridge which connected the lake with the old town harbour and the sea as Spyros led Popi to a taverna table. They sat taking in the scene, each nursing an ice-cold beer. Soon their skewers of juicy pork souvlaki arrived accompanied by bread and a salad. As they ate, Spyros' relaxed manner dissipated any feelings of anxiety in Popi over the endless paperwork. The food was delicious and when they had finished, it was hard to drag themselves up from their seats but in any case their departure was further delayed by the waiter bringing a plate of water melon, grapes and a carafaki of raki to enjoy. By the time they stood up to leave, it was the middle of the afternoon and they decided that when they got back to the village Spyros would try to contact some boatbuilders and Popi would write her letter of resignation to the university.

She was not looking forward to composing that letter. Although it was more easily done from afar, Popi was aware that it was cutting a tie with her former life. She had worked hard to get her university post and now she was leaving all that behind her. Had she been seduced by the beauty of the island? She reassured herself that her proposed business would easily satisfy her love of the sea as much as her academic career had done. As they climbed the coast road away from Agios Nikolaos and she looked out of the car window at the bay of Mirabello, Popi could not conceive of a place more perfect to make a life. So what if the sun, sea and timeless allure of the mountains had turned her head? Here she felt alive, and for the first time in many years complete.

If the view going up the mountain was stunning, what met them as they topped the summit was a scene that transformed the sublime to the heavenly. In the distance the island of Spinalonga lay at anchor defending the northern approaches. In the afternoon light details were coming more into focus, colours had refreshed and shapes reasserted themselves after their bleaching in the noonday sun. Wakes from boats on their workaday trips to the island wove patterns on the azure counterpane as they descended the hill towards Elounda.

From the terrace in her village house, Popi surveyed the same view from a different perspective. Even through the mish mash of telephone poles, water tanks and solar panels, the little piece of paradise that confronted her was a reassurance as she sat typing a letter to the university.

*

If Popi was feeling buoyant, Spyros was struggling. Back at his own house, he had put in several calls to contacts at the marina at Agios Nikolaos, but had drawn a blank in trying to find a craftsman to finish the caique. Some did not have the skills to work with wood and any who might have could not start for months or even years. Without a boat their business was just a pipe dream.

Although Spyros had contacts who were carpenters, they might be able to help fitting out, but did not have the specialist skills to work on the hull. Not only was he beginning to despair of finding a master craftsman who was available, he was also starting to feel the weight of guilt that he would have to dash Popi's dreams. Perhaps he could try further afield, at marinas along the coast to the west, in the capital Heraklion, or Rethymnon, even Chania, though they were far away and unlikely to produce any results. Still, he would not give up, he would do some research that evening and make some calls tomorrow.

'Oh no!' Spyros jumped from his chair.

'What is it Spyro?' a startled Thea asked her husband.

'Popi's writing her resignation. I must get to her before she sends it to the university, in case I cannot find a boatbuilder.'

He dialled her number on his phone but, as was often the case in the village, he had no signal. Spyros set out through the village lanes leaving the door open behind him. As he reached Popi's house he was just in time to find her coming out carrying her laptop.

'I'm off to Elounda to find a cafe with wifi to email my letter. Do you want to come?'

'That's why I came to see you. I think you should hold off a bit with your resignation.'

'Is there a problem?' Popi seemed crestfallen.

'Well, maybe just a hiccough,' said Spyros trying to soften the blow.

The young woman reached for her key and reopened her front door.

'Come inside and tell me about it.'

Spyros recounted the trouble he was having finding a craftsman to take on the task of finishing the caique. He reassured Popi that the next day he would try further afield, but both of them agreed this was not ideal. They would probably have to transport the boat a long way and would be unable to keep a close eye on the build. As an architect, Spyros knew how important it was to be hands-on with a project, and emotionally it was important for Popi to keep a close attachment to her father's legacy.

'Perhaps if we wait a few weeks we'll have more options, when most of the boats in Agios Nikolaos are back in the water,' said Popi. 'Didn't Costas say this was the busiest time?' As the words fell from her mouth, something clicked. Spyros immediately understood what she was thinking and it unsettled him.

'Why don't we ask Costas?' Popi saw from her uncle's expression that he was not keen on the suggestion. 'Come on, uncle, you said yourself that my father thought he was a good craftsman.'

The thought had already occurred to Spyros but he had dismissed it, feeling Costas' involvement with their business could only lead to trouble. But perhaps, if it was their only option and nobody raked over the past, it could work.

'What a great idea. I should have thought of it earlier.'

A smile tried to cover the reluctance Syros felt. It did not go unnoticed by his niece, but Popi's relief at maybe having found a solution wiped away any glimmer of disquiet she felt.

'I don't have an address for him, but he will be working at the marina. I have meetings with clients for the next couple of days, but maybe after that…'

'I can go.' Popi did not know whether it was her craving to find someone to finish the caique or something else which made her impatient to try and find the young man she had not known since she was a child, but now the offer had been made.

'Why not?' Spyros said. He reasoned that if they were going to work with Costas, Popi would certainly have to get to know her father's ex-apprentice. Judging from his demeanour late on the night of the funeral, he guessed that Costas would be reluctant to talk about the past.

*

Early the next morning, flushed with optimism about her new business tinged with nervousness about approaching Costas, Popi headed down the mountain road. She tried to concentrate on navigating the harbour front, as new friends, some of whom she recognised from her father's funeral, waved greetings to her. Leaving Elounda behind her, the road climbed and she had to drop into second gear to make the summit. The view down to Agios Nikolaos from the top of the mountain was glorious that morning. The sun glinted off the bay of Mirabello as a huge cruise liner manoeuvred towards the improbably small quay.

87

Despite the early hour, Popi was reluctant to drive through the narrow streets of the town, and her uncle had suggested she park her car at the port and walk from there to the marina. Slowly she made her way around the one way system that crossed the headland cutting back to where the giant ship was making landfall.

With relief she pulled into a space beside a striking statue. She could not remember it being there when she had visited as a child. Reading the name of the giant bronze, the *Abduction of Europa*, brought back memories of the legend she had learned in the village school all those years ago.

She could recognise that the statue depicted Europa, the daughter of the Phoenician king Agenor, sitting on the god Zeus in the form of a bull. If she remembered the story correctly, when word of Europa's charms reached the god he was determined to seduce her. Transforming himself into a white bull, he passed unnoticed amongst Agenor's grazing herds. In this disguise he won the trust of the young beauty and, coaxing her to climb on his back, swam with her to Crete where they came ashore at Matala on the south coast. Here, beneath the sandstone cliffs on that tamarisk-shaded beach they emerged from the waves, Europa to become the first Queen of Crete. Zeus and Europa parented three sons, Rhadamanthus, Sarpedon and Minos. As such, their union was not only responsible for the great Minoan civilisation but Europa also gave her name to the continent of Europe.

A welcome breeze tousled her hair as she set out along the coast road towards the marina. Before her on the headland stood another statue, one she did remember from her childhood. She pondered on how long she had been away from her homeland, and the thought made her nervous about meeting with Costas, who was all but a stranger to her.

As she walked towards the glass and copper structure, its name came back to her: *Cornucopia*, the horn of plenty given in gratitude by the god Zeus to his nursemaid the goat Almathea. To Popi, looking up as the sunshine bounced off the statue, it represented the relationship between the land, the sea and sunlight which provided for Crete and her people. Somehow the power of eternal plenty she saw in the statue raised her spirits. She stepped out with more confidence past the still-deserted small beach of Kritoplatia. Some tables around the bay were taken by people stopping for coffee on their way to work or tourists stopping to fuel up on a cooked breakfast. Popi was tempted to stop too as she had forgone food to make an early start. No, she should find Costas first, and then maybe she would find something to eat.

The tinkling of halyards on masts told her she was nearing the marina. Despite the early hour people were aboard boats washing, sanding, varnishing, or preparing their sails for sea. Alongside the car park a number of vessels stood out of the water, propped up on the hard standing. Several looked in a sorry condition, holes gaping in their sides, paint flaking to expose the scarred wood beneath. The vans of marine engineers sat in the shade of plastic-hulled cabin cruisers as their owners sweated to service their huge engines.

'Costa?'

The tall, muscular man wielding a paintbrush turned. A drop of blue paint ran off the brush and down his hand as he stared momentarily.

'Popi.' His uncertain smile turned to a worried frown as he tried to understand why on earth she should be there.

'Can we talk?'

Costas was not sure he wanted to talk, but on the other hand there was something that drew him towards the smiling girl who, prior to the other night, he had not seen for 10 years. Surely she could do him no harm, but he needed some time to compose his thoughts.

'I'm busy at the moment.'

'Maybe you'll not be so busy later? When do you stop for lunch?'

'I work for myself, so I stop when I want.' Costas could see she was not going to give up easily, and there was something about her that made him feel lunch with Popi would not be so awful.

'And when might you think you'll want to stop?'

Turning towards the half-painted hull he considered whether to take this step or not. She seemed friendly enough, as she had the other night. If Popi had been mad at him he was sure he would have sensed it in her demeanour. Could it hurt to have lunch with this attractive girl? As he stared at the unfinished hull, curiosity got the better of him.

*

Popi waited in the small taverna staring out to sea, sipping a cool glass of lemonade. It was already half an hour after Costas had agreed to meet her. She told herself that this was not unusual, but what if he had decided not to come? She was disappointed at the thought as it would scupper all her plans, but there was something else inside her that made her want to see him again. Why had she sensed reluctance in Costas to meet with her?

The taverna owner approached, asking if she would like to order any food. Looking at her watch, Popi reached for the menu and had just chosen the stuffed tomatoes and peppers when a blushing Costas arrived.

'I'm sorry I'm so late.'

'*Mia birra, parakalo*.' Ordering a beer as he sat down, he explained that he did not conform to the Greek stereotype for lack of punctuality, but that the owner of the boat had turned up to discuss the work he still wanted doing and had kept him talking.

'You understand, I need the work, so had to stay and discuss it.'

'It's not a problem.' Popi's smile put the young man at ease. 'I hope you don't mind, but I have just ordered, I was starving.'

'*Kotopoulo me patates*,' Costas mouthed towards the taverna owner. 'Chicken and potatoes, I always eat the same for lunch. It saves me thinking of what to order and it's quick if I'm busy as it's already cooked and on the hot plate.'

'*Stin ya sas*, to your health Costa.' The owner placed a beer in front of the boatbuilder and Costas raised it from the table. '*Yamas* Popi. It's good to see you again after all this time. I'm sorry it is in such tragic circumstances.' As Costas smiled, his face lit up and his eyes glinted. His gaze made her feel self-conscious. Popi lifted a hand to her cheek to sweep aside a lock of dark hair which had dropped over one eye.

Both of them were eager to move the conversation on. When Costas asked her about her life in England, Popi was happy to make small talk, putting off broaching the real reason for her meeting with him. Costas talked about how he missed working in wood, building traditional boats with his bare hands. When he spoke of his erstwhile

92

craft he became animated, as though a weight had been lifted from his shoulders. As they both finished eating, a lull in their chat prompted Costas to fill the silence.

'It really is lovely to see you Popi, but I'm intrigued why you wanted to meet with me?'

Popi took a deep breath.

'Well, I know my father always thought you had talent for boatbuilding.' She saw Costas look down, finding it hard to receive the compliment.

'The thing is, I would like you to consider finishing the caique.'

As soon as she had spoken she was aware of a mist falling over the young man's face.

Costas looked up from the floor. 'What caique?' If he had blushed slightly with embarrassment at the earlier praise, his face was now drained of some of its colour.

'The caique sitting in my olive grove, the one he was building for the rich customer who pulled out and made the business go bust.'

'I don't understand. What is it doing up in the village?'

Costas seemed shocked that the half-built boat still existed, and amazed that it was sitting in the village where he used to live.

'My father and uncle towed it up there when the boatyard closed. It was all he had left. I think he had dreams of completing the boat sometime, but then he died. I want to finish it and start up an ecological boat tour business. It will be a lasting memorial to Dad and means that I can stay in Greece. Please, Costa, can you help me?'

The look on the young woman's face nearly swayed Costas to go against his better judgement and agree to take on the task. Even in the short time they had been eating together he had felt attracted to Popi. Not only was she beautiful but she reminded him of the happier times of his youth. He considered what she had said to him. Perhaps he could turn the clock back. After all, he loved using the skills he had learned from Manolis and there were few opportunities to use them these days. He bought himself time.

'Let me think about it. Give me your number and I will ring you tomorrow.'

Costas was dying to finish the discussion after exchanging numbers and made his excuses, saying he was busy and had to get back to work.

As he left, Popi was unsure what to think. She found Costas impossible to read. She liked him, but he seemed to be holding something back. She had seen his love for his craft shining through, and if she had read the signals right even thought that he might like her a little, but she sensed deep within him nestled some unhappiness.

Driving back to Elounda, she remembered how her father had seen building boats not merely as a trade, but a vocation. When Costas talked about working with wooden vessels again she had recognised the same light in his eyes. Why then would he not leap at the opportunity to take on the project? Was the attraction she now felt for someone she barely knew, blinding her judgment? Was her desire to finish the caique stopping her from seeing that other people might not share her dream? Had she scared Costas off by being too forward?

Churning these thoughts around in her head, by the time she reached the square in Elounda she realised she had no recollection of the drive. It concerned her that the fine views of the sea from the cliffside road had not registered. She had come all this way without enjoying the drive or appreciating its dangers. She blinked and shook her head as she turned onto the road to the village.

Parking under the shade of a tree beside the church, she decided to take a walk to clear her head. She was in Crete now; things would happen but she would have to let them take their course. Patience was something she needed to learn. The streets of the village were deserted; shutters were closed against the afternoon heat which had stirred the orchestra of cicadas into a full-voiced chorus. Out of the walls of dilapidated houses geraniums bloomed and a small fig tree sprouted from the stone track.

Looking upwards, Popi had to bend her head right back to see the peak of the mountains that towered above her, the silhouettes of solitary trees peering down from their precarious perches on the shoulders of the summit to the olive groves of the valley. She sat on a dry-stone wall and a lizard scuttled away to find refuge in a crack. The tranquillity calmed her anxiety. She felt she could have remained sitting on the wall for eternity, but the heat drove her back to the refuge of her house. Closing the blue shutters, she collapsed on the bed and succumbed to a dreamless siesta.

The ring of her mobile phone awoke her. Spyros was intent on knowing how she had got on in Agios Nikolaos.

'Come down to the house and you can tell me all about it.'

As Popi left her new home to walk to her aunt and uncle's cottage she could see the brilliant blue triangle of the bay surrounded by mountains. Somehow she must find a way for her dream to become a reality so she could remain in this place where she felt so much at home.

Sitting on the terrace, Popi recounted her conversation with Costas to her uncle. He was unsurprised that the young boatbuilder had needed time to think about the proposal. In his own heart he was unsure how he felt. On the one hand, he would be pleased if they found someone to take on the work; but he was not sure that Costas was the right person. Still, the outcome now lay in the lap of the gods. Perhaps he was worrying unnecessarily.

It had just gone 8 o'clock the following morning when Popi's phone rang. Seeing Costas' name on the screen, she took a deep breath and accepted the call. Costas said he made no promises but would like to come and see what state the boat was in before he made a decision. Popi found it hard not to be excited. He was at the very least considering her proposal and wanted to meet with her in an hour's time.

She ran down the hill to her aunt and uncle's house but Thea told her Spyros had already left to see a client in Heraklion and would not be back until later that afternoon.

'I'm sure your uncle won't mind if you meet with Costas alone again. He's as excited about getting things underway as you are,' encouraged Thea.

Buoyed up by her aunt's support, Popi returned home to await Costas. Why did the minutes tick by so slowly and what was it that made her so nervous? She consciously tried to slow down her breathing. Was her anxiety born purely out of her desire to get her boat finished or was there something else at play? Popi did not examine these feelings too deeply and diverted herself by thinking what she might do if Costas refused to help.

As 9 o'clock came and went, Popi could not stop herself looking at her watch every few seconds. Perhaps Costas had changed his mind. Just a quarter of an hour later she ran to answer the knock at the door.

'Sorry if I'm a bit late, I had to stop for petrol for my scooter and got chatting.' Costas smiled apologetically.

'You're not late. I was just making a coffee. Would you like one?'

'No, but a glass of water would be good.'

'Perhaps I'll just have water too; it is starting to get quite hot.' Popi quickly poured two glasses. She was longing to get on with showing Costas the boat. 'Would you like to take a look at the caique?'

'Lead the way.' Costas followed as Popi went out of the door to the terrace stepping down into the olive grove. He stopped when he saw the skeleton of the boat chocked up beneath the olive trees. He had not known what he would feel when he saw the boat after all these years. Should he have come here at all? As he looked from the boat to Popi and back again his reluctance began to shift. Both were exquisite. He walked towards the frame of the caique, unable to stop smiling.

He had forgotten the elegance of the lines that his former employer had been able to craft from his imagination. Costas ran his hands over the smoothed wood, every joint was perfect and the years sat under the olive tree had not detracted from the perfection he now remembered. As he took in every detail of the frame Popi could see the craftsman's eyes light up.

Transfixed by the classic boat, Costas knew at once he could not pass up the opportunity to do the work. He might never get the chance again to use his traditional skills. He looked at Popi and any reservations he might have had were sunk.

'Beautiful.' Costas murmured.

Popi felt herself blushing.

'She's beautiful.' The boatbuilder tapped his hands on the stempost. 'I would love to finish the boat, if you will have me?'

'Thank you. I would like that very much.' Popi found herself unable to stop grinning.

'I could start in about a week's time if that's not too long for you to wait. My work at the marina is getting a bit thin on the ground now it's spring and owners are using their boats.'

'That's fantastic. It will give us time to agree payment and order in the materials you need to make a start. I need to talk to my uncle Spyros as he is in partnership with me and supplying the money.'

Popi noticed Costas glance at the floor. 'Will that be OK?'

'Are you sure your uncle consents to me doing the job?'

Costas looked worried, as though his chance to work on the boat was being snatched from his grasp.

'Why wouldn't he be? He knows I'm asking you and he's as eager as I am to get the boat afloat.'

'If that's the case then I think we have a deal. Have you got a pencil and some paper? If you like I could start making a list of the timber I'll need to start off with. I'm sure we can agree terms after you've spoken with Spyros.'

Returning from indoors with a pencil and paper, Popi saw Costas kneeling to examine the wood of the keel. She stopped to watch as something caught his eye and he ran his hand gently over the sturdy timber. Looking up, he caught Popi's gaze and smiled.

'We'll have *Katerina* in the water by the end of summer.'

Popi looked shocked. Why had Costas called the boat that? Seeing her face fall he called her to him.

'Look here, carved in the keel.'

Popi bent her head down to examine the wood. Chiselled out of the copper-coloured iroko was her mother's name.

Chapter 6

THE REALISATION THAT Manolis had named the boat after her mother came as a shock to Popi. As she traced her fingers over the inscription on the keel she could not help thinking of what might have been. Even in the depths of his despair and with his marriage falling apart around him he had still loved his wife. With their affection running so deep, what would it have taken to save their marriage? Katerina and Popi's life could have been so different and perhaps her father might not have died.

The tears ran down her cheeks dropping onto the parched wood of the keel. For Costas it also reminded him of the days of his apprenticeship with the kind boatbuilder who had taken him on and taught him all he knew of his trade. Embarrassed, he looked to the ground. He couldn't bear to see Popi so upset. He hardly knew her, but already he felt a strong connection to the delightful young woman who he remembered as a child.

'I'm sorry. That was insensitive of me. I shouldn't have shown you.'

Popi felt a strong arm placed hesitantly around her shoulders.

'No, it's OK. It's just that… it makes me think of what life could have been like if Mum and Dad had stayed together. How, if their love was so strong, their marriage proved so weak.'

Costas said nothing but drew her into his chest until the tears subsided. He should have thought before showing her the inscription. In his excitement about the prospect of working on the boat he had not considered Popi's feelings. Was it really a good idea for him to work with her on the caique? It had taken him 10 years to put the past behind him and, for Manolis' daughter, the boat had brought the past back to haunt her.

Guiding her away, they sat in the shade of an olive tree. Popi looked around at the blackened gnarled trunk so deeply rooted in the earth, its size betraying its presence here for countless generations. On the slopes of the grove were hundreds of such trees clinging to the mountainside all the way down to the bay, a view which Popi knew had remained the same for thousands of years. Somehow that thought comforted her and, as she leant her head onto Costas' chest, her mind began to clear.

'Thank you, Costa, I'm pleased you discovered it.'

In Popi's mind the boat had now taken on an even deeper significance. It was no longer just a memorial to her dad but a symbol of the love between her mother and father.

'Let's go inside and I'll fix us that coffee and we can make a list.'

*

With the keel, stem and sternposts fashioned from sturdy north African iroko, Costas suggested they use traditional pine for the ribs and planking, fixed with stainless steel fastenings and caulked with cotton. If they ordered these materials he could finish the *petsoma*, or planking the hull, Popi could help with the painting and they could decide on the engine and materials for the deck, cabin and interior later.

Costas kept going outside to take measurements and as the list grew Popi began to understand the magnitude of what they had taken on. The young boatbuilder seemed more excited than daunted, and the deeper they got into the task the more animated he became. Any reticence Popi had noticed before seemed to have vanished as Costas warmed to the job of planning the build.

It was early afternoon before the pair realised they had not stopped for lunch and, looking down at the list, Popi was concerned about the budget and what her uncle would think of the cost. They agreed to go to the taverna and await Spyros' return from Heraklion later.

They were hungrier than they thought and found it difficult to resist ordering a number of mezzes from the menu: local spicy sausage, creamy cheese croquettes, small skewers of pork souvlaki, a country omelette with horta and salad. Somehow a carafe of cold red wine was squeezed onto the table as the couple toasted their new partnership.

Over lunch, Popi expanded upon her plans for the caique. Costas could see her eyes glinting as she told him about her proposals for setting up her 'Underwater Safaris' and 'Stars and Legends' cruises. Her ideas were good and Costas did not want to dampen her enthusiasm by suggesting how difficult it was to earn a living in Crete at the moment. Nobody else was offering such tours, and maybe if she could do a few deals with some of the larger hotels she could make a go of it.

When they could eat and drink no more and were about to leave, Popi's phone rang. Spyros was back and anxious to know how his niece had got on.

'Shall we come to your house and talk you through it?'

'We?'

'Costas is still with me.'

'Come on up.'

Costas seemed reluctant. 'I really should be getting back.'

'Come on, Costa, if we can sort out the finances and agree the order we can get started as soon as possible. I thought you were keen to get going.'

Popi was right, Costas thought, and her uncle did know she was asking him to build the boat. Perhaps he was worrying needlessly.

'I suppose it won't matter if I get home later.' Hanging back, Costas followed Popi through the village lanes.

On the drive from Heraklion, Spyros had found himself hoping that Popi had managed to persuade Costas to help. If he had his doubts, he was prepared to put them aside to help his niece. By the time they arrived at his front door he had convinced himself to forget whatever had gone before and welcomed Costas with a warm handshake. Popi noticed him visibly relax as her uncle shepherded them outside onto the terrace.

Spyros was generous in his offer of wages and did not seem to be put off by the list Popi and Costas had prepared. They agreed that he should source the wood through his business contacts whilst Costas ordered fixings, caulking and paint at a chandlery shop in Agios Nikolaos. All the receipts were to be passed to Popi who would keep the accounts and manage the build.

Carrying a tray, Thea came outside with a carafe of raki and four glasses for them to toast the new business venture. Popi told her aunt and uncle how Costas had found her mother's name chiselled into the keel. In the telling she was no longer upset by the discovery but rather spurred on to succeed by its poignancy, though Thea became as tearful as she had earlier.

'We couldn't change the name of the boat anyway, it would be bad luck. I think your sister-in-law would be proud to have the caique named after her,' Spyros said gently. 'Whatever went between them, she really loved Manolis. They had Popi together.' He turned to his niece and for a moment held her gaze. 'And you are her world. She would not roll back the past to change that for anything.'

Popi blushed slightly and raised her glass.

'To Mum. To Katerina. *Yamas*.'

Popi was impatient to get started on the build but her uncle said it would be some days at the earliest before the first order of timber could be delivered. Costas thought the chandlers would have enough fixings in store to get him started as soon as the wood arrived. He had a couple of days' work to finish off at the marina but could schedule those around their plans.

Seeing Popi was intent on keeping the momentum of the business going, her uncle offered her the use of his caique so she could get afloat and start planning her tours. Although this might be a little premature, it would stop her from bursting with impatience as they waited for the building to start. He knew she was a competent skipper and that his treasured boat would be safe in her hands.

*

Despite his work commitments, over the next few days Costas spent a lot of time at Popi's house. He spent hours outside in the olive grove taking measurements and making notes. On his motor scooter he ferried up tools and a tarpaulin which he tied to branches of the trees to form a makeshift canopy over the boat. Extension leads were rolled out to provide power for his tools and he washed the frame thoroughly before letting it dry in the sunshine and painting it in an orange-coloured protective primer. It seemed as though he was as impatient to begin the work as the owner of the boat.

In the meantime, Popi took note of the expenditure in a ledger, sorted out the receipts Costas gave her and filed them away in a tin. When he was there she would make him coffee which they drank together on the terrace and she would take him water as he worked measuring or painting the frame.

She had never seen anyone - since her father when she was a child - so engrossed in his work. As Costas ran his hands or paintbrush over the sleek bones of the craft he seemed to have all the time in the world. Any impatience he showed at wanting to get to work was dissipated by his absorption in the task itself. The first few times she had met up with him since returning to Crete, she had sensed something was troubling him. Perhaps she had been imagining it, or perhaps it was just shyness, but as she watched him working on the boat, alone beneath the olive trees, she could not imagine anyone more content with himself.

As a girl she had always liked the shy apprentice that her father had taken on. Already tall, he was wiry and had seemed unsure in his own body. Now as she watched him work he was confident. His long, dark hair pulled back, in the heat he had pulled down the top of his overalls and tied the sleeves around his waist revealing a strong, muscular body. If Popi had been grateful to this handsome man for helping make her dream of finishing the boat come true, perhaps she was now feeling something more about being near Costas.

Turning to open a new tin of paint, Costas momentarily caught the eye of Popi who was sitting in the shade of an olive tree writing in her notebook. Quickly she glanced back down. Had he seen her watching him? He was too far away to notice her redden but she had clearly seen his face open to a smile before she averted her look. Popi was not sure if it was seeing her father's boat being brought to life or something else, but she was aware of feeling self-conscious under the gaze of his glinting brown eyes.

As Costas worked, he felt himself relax. How long had it been since he had felt this happy? He was at last back to doing something he loved, using the traditional crafts he had learned from Manolis all those years ago. Looking through the olive groves down to the bay as he worked cleaning and painting the boat, he thought that maybe he was the happiest man alive. Had he imagined it, or had he caught Popi staring at him as he worked? Dare he believe that this alluring woman who had turned his life around might have feelings for him? Perhaps that was in his imagination, but even the thought of it enhanced his mood.

By the end of those few days, Costas was disappointed to discover he had done all he could until the first delivery of timber arrived. With there being no need for him to come to the house the following day, Popi decided to take up her uncle's offer to use his boat and do a detailed exploration of the coast to find suitable destinations for her proposed cruises.

As she lay in bed that night she found it hard to sleep as she thought of possible places she should explore, where the best places to snorkel were and which beaches could she take visitors to watch the night sky. But there was something else keeping her awake. Why didn't she ask Costas to come with her? He had no work until the wood was delivered. Although she felt scared of asking her new friend, she also felt a tingle of excitement at the prospect. By the time she slipped into sleep she had decided she would invite Costas along on the trip.

In the clear light of the new morning she felt her resolve foundering. Although she had seen how happy he was whilst working on the boat she had also been aware of his awkwardness around her when they first met and his initial reluctance to get involved in the project. She found the enigmatic boatbuilder difficult to read. All her future plans were dependent on Costas finishing the boat. If she scared him off, her hopes of staying on Crete would be scuppered. She decided it would be best to go out on her own and not put her future in jeopardy on a notion there might be something more to her relationship with Costas than there was.

She stuffed a bag with a swimming costume, change of clothes, towels and notebook. She would buy food and drink from the shops in Elounda before setting out. She phoned her uncle to check it was OK to take the boat and if she could pop in to pick up the keys. Spyros was pleased for his niece to get out to sea. He loved to see her so cheerful.

'Do you know how far you will be going and for how long?' he enquired. 'It's just that if you are going out into the bay of Mirabello, you might want to consider getting a new chart as mine are terribly out of date. Those are my spare keys, hang on to them and use the boat whenever you want. Just make sure you keep it topped up with diesel.'

'I was thinking of heading out to Mirabello. I might stay out this evening to explore beaches for the star gazing too.'

To find a chart she would now have to go to Agios Nikolaos which would seriously eat into her day of planning. She had told herself she would not be inviting Costas on the trip but, if he could get a chart in the town and bring it to her, then surely it would be alright to ask him along?

Taking her phone from her pocket she turned to Spyros.

'Do you mind if I ask Costas to come with me?'

She noticed her uncle hesitate.

'Of course I don't mind, it'll make handling the boat a bit easier if there are two of you.'

Popi punched in the number as she walked outside to the terrace and paused momentarily before pushing dial. She barely gave time for Costas to give a cursory greeting before asking him if he would like to come, quickly qualifying her invitation with her need for the new chart.

'I have nothing on now. I've not taken any new work in order to work on the caique. I'd love to come.' Costas tried to hide his pleasure at the unexpected invitation. 'Would you like me to bring anything other than the chart?'

'I'll buy us food and some drinks in Elounda. Can you be at my uncle's boat in two hours?'

'See you there.'

As Costas hung up, Popi knew that if she examined her reasons for asking him to get the chart, they would not bear too much scrutiny. But she did feel glad, even excited so did not allow her mind to follow that route.

'Here are the keys.' The corners of Spyros mouth turned up into a slight smile as he caught the glint in Popi's eye as she turned to leave.

'*Efharisto*, thanks Uncle, I'll keep her safe for you.'

Spyros had no doubts about the safety of his boat, it was Popi who he didn't want to see hurt. But for the moment she seemed content, and that made him feel good.

*

On the waterfront, fishermen mended nets and sold their overnight catches from the quay beside their moored boats. Popi wove her way around the cats gathered in the hope of scraps as she crossed the road to the shops to buy provisions. When she returned to the harbour-side Costas had already arrived, a good half hour early. Sitting astride his scooter, he opened the top box behind him and waved the chart.

'I got one.' Stepping from the bike he locked the crash helmet that was slung from the handlebars in the box.

'I'm early for a change,' he said smiling, as he took in Popi, dressed in shorts, t-shirt and flip flops.

'Come aboard.' Popi tugged at the mooring rope to pull the bow nearer to the quay and Costas stepped onto the deck then pulled on the same hawser to narrow the gap for Popi. After stowing the food and drink in the cool box they unpacked the sun canopy from a cockpit locker and rigged it over the boom. As Popi started the engine and took the tiller, Costas went forward to cast off. Moving slowly astern she slipped the mooring and reversed into the pool of the harbour. The caique painted a wide circle on the dark blue canvas of the enclosed waters as Popi steered forwards, out into Korfos.

It was nearly noon and the bay was busy with boats making their way to and from Spinalonga. Although a sea breeze was starting to blow as the land soaked up the scorching heat of the midday sun, Popi was confident about taking the caique out through the channel between Spinalonga and Kalidon into the open waters of the Aegean. Taking that route would save them having to lower the mast to get under the bridge at the southern entrance to the bay.

As the boat sailed into open sea it took on a comfortable roll in rhythm with the dance of the waves, its broad beam riding the swell with comfort. Both caique and skipper seemed at one with the undulating waters as, smiling, Popi swept the hair from her eyes and

113

fixed her gaze on the course ahead. Costas came astern to the cockpit and under the awning stripped off his shirt, for a moment diverting Popi's gaze from where she was steering. Something else caught her eye; to seaward of the boat a silver flying fish leaped clear of the water.

'Look, there!'

Others in the shoal joined in flitting above the waves before diving, only to re-emerge with the most prodigious leaps as they darted across the rolling surface of the water. For several minutes the fish played around the boat, the sun glinting off their silver wings, then all of a suddens they disappeared.

Popi glided the boat into the gulf of Exo Vathi, but noted that the steep rocks that surrounded the inlet might make it dangerous for inexperienced swimmers so struck it off her list of possible dive sites. To the south on a headland she spotted the small church of Agios Fokas. She remembered her father telling her that it was here more than ten centuries ago that the Byzantine fleet had moored after sailing to Crete from Constantinople to liberate the island from the Saracens.

Leaving Kolokytha island to port she manoeuvred into a bay, Popi recalled that this was a good spot for snorkelling but that it also got crowded as the big tourist boats from Agios Nikolaos would often stop here for barbecues on their way back from day trips to

Spinalonga. In the evening however it would be deserted and a possible location for her 'Stars and Legends' cruise.

Rounding Cape Vagia, the southern point of Kalidon, Popi set course for the canal at Poros. Even in the lee of the peninsula she knew the rolling waves would make seeing the lost city of Olous unlikely, but she would keep it on her list for calmer days.

Being at the helm of her uncle's boat, Popi felt a sense of freedom that she had rarely experienced since childhood. Even in the swell that crinkled the open water she remained assured, at one with the movement of the boat. But there was something playing on her mind, a pull stronger than that of the wind or the waves. Standing at the tiller, she felt herself transported back to the days when she would take to the water with her dad. To the days before their world fell apart. She knew where she wanted to go: a place that would bring back memories of those happy times.

What was stopping her from swinging the helm over and setting a course for the beach? She remembered her father telling her that it was their secret and that the secret cove belonged to the turtles. But now her father was dead, could it hurt to return to the spot they so cherished together? Looking across the cockpit, she caught Costas looking at her, his eyes smiling as he leant back on the cabin bulkhead. Popi felt a warm glow inside; Costas grinned as she caught his gaze, but he did not look away. Laughing, Popi was convinced she could trust him to keep her secret. She remembered her father had always liked his apprentice and never had a bad word to say about him.

Letting the crest of a wave pass under the hull, she waited to settle into the trough and pushed the rudder over using both hands, squinting, she scanned the mountainside for the small white church she could use as a waypoint to get near the distant cove. Costas smiled as he saw Popi change direction. He did not say anything as he noticed the helmswoman's gaze fix on the chapel on the hill.

In the swell she would lose sight of the landmark as the caique pitched down into the troughs of the waves. Popi glanced down at the compass mounted on gimbals in front of her and took note of the bearing she should steer to. Costas wondered whether he should offer to take a stint at the helm but as he stared at the young woman, her face set into the wind, her long dark hair blowing in the breeze and her sparkling eyes intent on the course he could not have been more content than just to watch her.

The caique made easy work of the rumbling seas and Popi felt a warm glow of pride when she recollected it was her father who had built the boat from a design he kept in his head. She thought how those same skills had been applied to the caique which was now hers and waiting to be finished beneath the olive trees in the grove beside her new home.

Glancing towards Costas she could see how comfortable he was with his surroundings; when he moved around the caique he seemed as at one with its movements as the vessel was with the wiles of the sea. At that moment she knew she had made the right choice to ask him to finish the boat. She turned and looked back, the richest of blue seas unrolling all the way to the horizon. Comfortable at the helm, Popi was attuned to the patches of ruffled grey which rode the waves as the flurries of wind rushed towards her. As each gust hit, she steadied her grip on the tiller to keep the boat on course.

As the afternoon sun began to cool, the wind adopted a calmer humour. Costas went below, returning with tins of cold drinks from the cool box, handing one to Popi. Ahead the sea now looked as though it had been smoothed by a giant hand and she could see the arms of land which cradled the secret cove. It was just as she had remembered. Popi slowed the engine so it was barely ticking over as the boat passed between the headlands and the full splendour of the cove was revealed.

It was from up on top of those sheer cliffs that Popi had peered down on the day of her father's funeral. A handful of tamarisk trees dotted the golden sands of the beach, sheltered by two rocky capes which almost closed the circle of the bay. Popi slowly steered the caique towards the tip of one of the jagged peninsulas before handing the helm to Costas. Taking off her t-shirt, Popi moved

117

forward and took the coiled bow line in hand before diving into the calm waters. Carefully climbing the rocky shoreline, she secured the rope around the base of a boulder before swimming back to the boat.

Costas dropped a rope boarding ladder over the side before putting out an anchor astern. As Popi climbed back aboard he cut the engine. The silence was deafening. Dripping, Popi sat down on the bench seat in the cockpit. Memories of the happy times she had spent here with her dad hit her at almost the same time as those of the last day she saw him alive. The confusion she felt inside cast a veil over the joy she had hoped her return to the cove would evoke. When she had been at sea, she had felt such a strong force pulling her here. Had it been wrong to come back to a place which held such poignant memories?

Costas could see the fog of distraction in the young woman's eyes and instinctively sat down and moved to comfort her. She trembled slightly as he wrapped an arm around her wet shoulders.

'It's all right. I'm just being stupid.' A tear escaped down Popi's cheek. She hated feeling weak but was comforted by Costas' closeness. Momentarily she closed her eyes, letting the warmth of the sun soothe her as her mind tried to wrestle its way back to some sort of equilibrium.

Popi was aware of her disappointment as Costas dropped his arm and got up. Returning from the galley, he offered her a handful

118

of paper napkins. As Popi wiped her eyes he went below again, returning with a chilled bottle of wine and two glasses. Costas sat quietly as they sipped their drinks, lending a sympathetic ear as Popi unburdened herself of the conflict she felt about her past life on Crete. Revisiting the bay had brought them back to the surface. Popi warmed to Costas' comforting presence as he gave her the space to try and explain her feelings, his few words enough to coax her sorrows into words. As they sat and talked, the secret bay worked its magic, soothing Popi's thoughts, coaxing her back to the present. The water of the bay was calm as mercury, silver grey as the light began to fade. Inland, the orange ball of the sun began its cool descent behind the mountains.

'I didn't realise how late it was getting.' Standing, Popi went to the cabin to get a fleece from her stash bag, bringing with her another bottle of wine.

'We haven't even eaten our picnic yet. I'm starving.' Passing a cool box through the hatch, they laid the table in the cockpit, not bothering with plates as they unwrapped ham, cheese, bread, pots of olives, tzatziki and beans, a bag of tomatoes, a cucumber and onions. As dusk fell slowly into nightfall the couple had found an easy space in each other's company, a moment neither wanted to end. Costas said nothing as Popi told him the story of the secret bay, about the turtles and how it had been a special place for her and her father. He

119

smiled at the thought of the tales Manolis must have told his daughter a decade ago and said little, allowing Popi time to come to terms with the memories her return there had rekindled. Costas was aware that it had been many years since he had experienced such a sense of contentment. Although the need for comfort had passed, as the chill of the evening took hold he put an arm around Popi's shoulder and drew her towards him for warmth. Turtle Beach had cast its spell and she thought how lucky she was to have found her way back here and to have met Costas again. The boatbuilder felt himself relax as he sensed the young woman snuggle to his chest.

Moored in the bay, both of them knew that it was getting late but neither wanted to broach the subject of their return to Elounda and by the time the first stars came out over the gently rocking waters of the lagoon the unsaid became an understanding that they would stay until dawn.

Chapter 7

AN EMPTY BERTH on the quay did not come as a surprise to Spyros when the following morning he strolled down to Elounda to buy bread. He had seen the way the young couple looked at each other. Despite any misgivings he might have, he was warming to Costas and was sure that the locals would remain silent to spare Popi's feelings. Now Manolis was dead, the past should be buried with him. If Popi and Costas had feelings for one another, it would be cruel if their love became another victim of past actions beyond their control.

Taking a seat in a cafe, Spyros ordered a coffee. He did not have long to wait before he spotted his caique entering the small harbour. The smiles on the faces of the young woman at the helm and her new lover standing on the foredeck confirmed they were fine. Spyros put some coins on the table and set off back up the hill to the village.

As Popi steered her uncle's boat back to its mooring she felt on cloud nine. After the night before, she was sure that Costas cared for her. His initial reluctance at wanting to get involved in her scheme to build the caique she put down to shyness. Standing at the bow, the boatbuilder also felt the warm glow of being loved. Any guilt he might have had about the past was banished by the pleasure he now felt. He was sure that the strength of their affection for one another could withstand anything.

Popi clung to Costas as the couple rode his motor scooter up the mountain road. The sight of a lorry unloading above the village reminded them of the wood delivery and they headed to the wall bordering Popi's olive grove, where Spyros was directing operations as timber was craned off the back of the large truck. Already piles of neatly stacked wood sat beside the skeleton of the boat beneath the makeshift canopy.

'I'm so sorry uncle, I forgot the delivery might come today,' Popi said as she removed the crash helmet Costas had given her to wear.

'It's no problem,' Spyros reassured her, 'I saw the lorry coming up the road from my terrace and I came over to make sure the wood was unloaded as close to the boat as possible.'

Popi could see the smile on Costas' face when he saw the wood being craned down onto the dry earth. She could see him mentally checking his list and running his hand across the planks and sheets of timber to ensure its quality. Somehow the delivery of the wood made their project seem very real and for Costas it signalled the start of a new chapter in his life.

For Popi, the sight of the neat stacks of wood took her back to the days when her father was beginning a new build. She remembered his face as he smiled in anticipation of crafting the boat. There was something in Costas' smile which reminded her of her dad's, and his expression gave her confidence that out of these piles of timber a new boat would emerge. To her, this caique meant more than any vessel she had ever encountered. This boat would anchor her to the ancient tradition of her family and hopefully help her build a future on the island.

Popi knew that Costas was aching to get started, but managed to persuade him to wait until she had served them lunch on the terrace. Reluctantly he acquiesced, agreeing that a break would give him time to gather his thoughts. As Popi talked to her uncle about possible places where she could take her boat tours, she was aware of Costas distractedly sketching on paper napkins with a stubby pencil he had retrieved from his trouser pocket.

'Go on then, I know you're aching to get started,' said Popi, laughing.

Costas grinned as he disappeared around the corner of the house into the olive grove, impatient to get his hands on the new wood and begin to cut, shape and smooth it into the boat he now held in his imagination. But as he approached the vessel, it was as though a switch had been flipped, slowing his breathing and turning his excitement into the patience he would need if the caique was to be the best he could make it.

By the time Popi and Spyros had finished their lunch and stepped into the olive grove to see how Costas was progressing, the neat piles of wood had been strewn around the shell of the vessel, each plank or sheet with a pencil mark denoting to which part of the hull Costas considered it most suitable. Spyros looked surprised at the mess but was reassured when Popi commented, 'It reminds me of dad's yard on the waterfront.'

Darkness was falling by the time Costas stopped work and returned to the house, tired and smiling, his shirt drenched in sweat.

'Let me put that through the wash while you have a shower, it will dry in no time on the line. Then I'll get us some dinner.'

Over their meal, Popi was enthralled by Costas' enthusiasm for building the boat. It was as though it had imbued his life with meaning. His natural reserve had been replaced by a passion that

124

made his whole being come alive. She was happy simply to listen to him talking, this time generously leaving the space into which the jumble of her new lover's thoughts could tumble.

Although it appeared that Costas' relish for the project could not be exhausted, his body succumbed to the tiredness his labours had caused and it was decided he should stay the night. So the couple fell into a pattern which saw their relationship slowly develop alongside the caique in the olive grove.

On some days it looked as though little progress had been made, but on closer inspection Popi could see small pieces of wood carefully jointed and fixed in place in readiness to support the larger timbers that were to follow. Other days it seemed that work had jumped ahead in leaps and bounds as the frame began to be covered in the skin which would form the outside of the hull.

Popi loved the time in the evening when she would round the corner of the house and see how the day's work had gone. In the moments before she went to look, the sense of anticipation was almost unbearable. As her caique grew daily out of the piles of wood in the olive grove, her affection for the man so lovingly crafting her dream flourished.

Sometimes she would stand at the corner of the house and watch Costas working. A spider's web of cables ran through the window to the boat. Occasionally she would hear the shriek of an electric saw or the shrill whirr of a drill, but mostly Costas worked in silence only resorting to power tools for the most rudimentary of work.

She stood entranced as he held up the planks of wood, running his eye along them, selecting the cuts with the most crooked grain to use for the strongest parts of the hull. These he lovingly cajoled using a *dovleti*, a combination of a hammer and adze, before firmly clamping and nailing into place.

Popi loved the sweet smell of the woodchips and resin from the pine mixed with the aromas of paint and turpentine mingling with the scents of herbs and wild-flowers blowing in off the mountains. Sometimes Costas could sense her stare and look up from his work smiling, and would take a break from his labours to explain how he was defining the shape of the hull by eye as he installed the ribands using a method which dated back to the time of classical Greece.

She watched as he would lie bare-chested on the parched ground, his arm outstretched, at one with the traditional *pirgoni* keyhole saw he wielded with such precision; or squatting down to sharpen a chisel with his pocket whetstone which he told her had been hewn from the veins of silicates mined in the surrounding hills.

Popi cherished those moments when the sun began to set and Costas would lead her around the boat, explaining what he had done that day. To be included this way in his passion for the work made her feel even closer to him. Afterwards, while Costas showered away the sweat of his day's labour, Popi would lay the table on the terrace. Later they would eat together looking down to the waters of the bay whilst Costas excitedly told her of his plans for the next day.

Some evenings he needed to return to his room in Agios Nikolaos, but often he would stay. On those perfect nights the couple would fall asleep exhausted in each other's arms, waking full of hope at what the new day would bring.

Often for Popi this would mean travelling to Agios Nikolaos and sometimes even Heraklion to try and secure the necessary commercial registrations and insurances for their new venture. She had got her mother to forward her certificates of competence as a skipper and in first aid, radio operating and sea survival from England. These needed to be translated into Greek before she could gain the required permissions to operate the business. The boat would also need to be inspected when it was completed, and Popi would also need a confirmatory assessment of her skills to satisfy the local authorities.

Spyros was as good as his word, providing the funds needed to pay the necessary fees and the costs of finishing the caique. When his business commitments allowed him time, he would accompany his niece and use his contacts to help navigate a path through the paperwork. Popi would also spend hours at her computer writing her scripts for the 'Stars and Legends' tours and pondering charts, seeking out the best options for her 'Underwater Safaris'.

When her plans were firmly in place, Popi worked closely with her uncle on the budget. Then she turned her attention to creating a website for the business and brochures to be given away in tour agencies and hotels. Keeping busy, the weeks passed quickly and with the hull fully planked and caulked the caique really was taking shape. Costas turned his attention to the topsides, building the cabin structure then laying the decks before lining the interior. When one evening over dinner the boatbuilder began to discuss the purchase of the engine, Popi thrilled at the thought that the end of the build was in sight. Spyros and Costas pored over piles of catalogues, discussing various technical specifications before placing an order for a suitable marine diesel.

While they awaited delivery of the engine, Costas spent the time plumbing, running wiring for the lights and navigation aids and fitting the propeller shaft in readiness to be connected. Meanwhile Popi was put to work painting the hull, the topsides a brilliant white and the bottom in blue anti-fouling. The decks were oiled and the cabin varnished both inside and out. Coat after coat of paint was added and meticulously sanded down before Costas was satisfied that the final finish could be applied.

The day before the engine was due to be delivered, the couple stood back and admired their work. It was only now, as she took pause in her labours, that Popi realised the true glory of the boat Costas had built for her. At that moment she thought it was the most wonderful caique she had ever seen. From stem to stern it was just perfect. Looking now at what had been achieved, a tear came to her eye as she thought of her father and the legacy they had created for him. Caught up in her thoughts, Popi did not notice Costas walk to the opening in the dry-stone wall where he had parked his scooter and take a paper parcel from the top box.

'I made these for you.' Popi turned to see him standing behind her holding out the package loosely tied up with string. Wiping her face on the back of her sleeve she reached out to accept the gift.

'What is it?' she asked, untying the bow which held the paper in place. As the wrapping fell away Popi was left holding two beautifully shaped plaques fashioned out of mahogany, her mother's name carved into each and then painted in gold.

'They're gorgeous.' Popi stared at the plaques, running her fingers over the grain into which the word 'Katerina' had been chiselled so lovingly. Carefully she placed them on the ground before turning to embrace Costas. Somehow these two simple pieces of wood expressed the welter of emotions she was now feeling. Popi didn't know if her tears were those of joy at the beauty of the caique

129

or sadness at the memory of her father and the breakdown of her parent's marriage.

'Here, I will fix them for you.'

Popi released Costas from her grasp and bent to pick up his gifts. Taking them over to the hull he climbed a ladder, carefully marking the bow of the hull before drilling and attaching the nameplates with screws then cutting wooden plugs to glue in the countersunk holes.

Returning to Popi's side she put her arm around his waist and drew Costas to her. 'Thank you,' was all she could find to say but the words made Costas glow inside.

The following morning, a clattering sound woke them from their slumbers, and the sound of Yiannis' voice reminded the couple that the garage owner had been enlisted by Spyros to help install the engine. Popi and Costas pulled on their clothes and ran to the olive grove to see Yiannis and one of his mechanics already standing beside the engine hoist they had unloaded from their truck.

'Sorry, did I wake you?' Yiannis smiled.

'Would you like a coffee?' Blushing, Popi headed indoors to the kitchen.

'I'd love one,' shouted Spyros, almost bumping into his niece as he rounded the corner of the house.

Sitting on the terrace, it was not long before they heard the grumbling sound of a lorry making its way up the hillside, pulling off the road into the olive grove through the gap in the wall. Directed loudly by Yiannis, the driver carefully manoeuvred his truck as close to the hull as possible before putting down the hydraulic supports and craning the engine to the ground.

The lorry gone, the four men took to attaching chains around the engine before hoisting it up and over the gunwales of the boat and swinging it over the cockpit until it hovered above the lined compartment Costas had built to house it in the bottom of the hull. Yiannis took control of operations on the ground while Costas carefully took charge as the engine was gingerly lowered into the specially constructed bay. The boatbuilder's smile betrayed his relief as the carefully aligned mounts took the weight off the chains and the engine was seated perfectly in the hull.

Lying on the cockpit floor, Yiannis and Costas methodically began connecting the wires, hoses, rods and shaft to the engine before lubricating all the moving parts and adding engine oil and coolant. It was late afternoon by the time Costas did his final checks to ensure all the skin fittings looked watertight and that the engine was ready for testing when the boat was launched.

That evening's meal took on something of a celebratory feel. Too tired to cook, with Yiannis and his mechanic joining them at the table, Popi went to the village taverna to order mezzes to take away. She returned laden with foil trays of souvlaki, village sausage, cheese croquettes, egg staka, horta omelette, stuffed vine leaves, baked haricot beans, Cretan salad, tzatziki and bread and set the food out on the terrace. They toasted the completion of the build with red wine and raki, and discussed the challenges of getting *Katerina* down the mountain to the water.

Popi was anxious at the thought of the boat being damaged on its precarious journey from the olive grove to the sea, but the men reassured her that Spyros' trailer was more than strong enough to take the weight of the caique. They would just have to take the drive down the mountain road at a snail's pace. Any traffic coming up the hill would have to find somewhere to pull over or reverse back down, while any following them would have to be patient. Launching the boat from the trailer would be easy; the most difficult task was getting the caique on the trailer from where it now rested. Yiannis again agreed to lend his help. Using his engine hoist and the motorised winch on Spyros' four-wheel drive, they were sure they could manoeuvre the hull onto the trailer.

It was agreed that they would attempt the journey in two days' time. Yiannis had work booked in at his garage the following day. Costas and Spyros wanted to visit the chandlers at Agios Nikolaos to look for a radio, GPS, echo sounder, fire extinguisher and other equipment required for the final fitting out.

The following morning, Popi was content to have some time on her own and indulged herself by cooking a breakfast of bacon, sausage, eggs and beans and eating it on the terrace. After taking her plate inside, she sat with her feet up on a chair, pondering what had brought her to this enchanting place. A new phase of her life was just beginning, and she couldn't wait for it to start. Tomorrow, if all went to plan, her boat would be in the water. Costas still had to wire in the new electrical devices, rig the short mast and mount the liferaft and lifebuoys, and the caique would be seaworthy.

She couldn't believe how relaxed she was in her surroundings. In her contentment, she realised that for the first time in her life she felt truly settled. In this house she had a place of her own, and if she could make a success of the business she would have enough money to get by. Then there was Costas. She smiled at the thought of her boyfriend, someone she remembered from her past on the island, who had come back into her life and stolen her heart. Out of the tragedy of her father's death had come all this, as though he was watching out for her from the skies, in a way he had been unable to do in life.

Clearing her mind, she stared down at the triangle of sea reflecting the light like glass before turning her gaze to the mountain, rocks scattered amongst the olive groves as though an ancient deity had coughed and set them free. The song of the cicadas grew louder in unison with the sun rising in the sky as shade was banished from the surrounding hills. She would have loved to have her mother there to share things with, but she too had found happiness with Andrew in England. She smiled at the thought of the two of them together and hoped that her mum was as content as she now was. It had been a long journey for both of them.

Alone, Popi felt the day spread out in front of her. Excited about the task ahead of them the following day, she felt the need to bridge the gap until tomorrow by doing something. Picking up a notebook and pen, she went outside into the olive grove and climbed the ladder that was propped against the side of her gleaming new boat. Passing through the companionway she descended the stairs to the cabin. She noted that all the wiring for the navigation instruments was in place, the galley was fitted out with a gimballed hob and cold cabinet but other than that the cabin looked bare. Costas was buying the essential equipment to make *Katerina* seaworthy but would not think of buying the bits and bobs which would make it practical and comfortable to spend time on.

She began writing: a few pots and pans, plates, cutlery, mugs, glasses, towels… the list went on. Already having filled a page, Popi realised she would need to satisfy herself by trying to make a few purchases that she knew were essential and then gradually equip the boat as she identified what was needed. Climbing down from the boat the strength of the sun hit her. She retreated inside the house to find a hat before closing the front door and setting off through the village lanes to the old donkey track which meandered downhill through the olive groves to the sea.

'*Kalimera.*' Popi returned the greetings of the group of elderly people sitting on rickety chairs outside the taverna, three women dressed in black and a man wearing a grey woollen jumper despite the scorching heat. The warmth of their welcome put a spring in her step as the stone surface of the path gave way to cobbles. In her soft-soled shoes she had to tread carefully so as not to turn an ankle, but she was in no rush, the views tempting her to savour every second of her walk.

A slight breeze whispered down the mountain, a silver ripple breaking the calm surface of a sea of olive leaves. A lone guard dog barked, his voice echoed in another village high above. Three goats heavy with milk looked up, bleating as Popi passed by. Entering the town the lanes led her to the harbour, her uncle's caique just one among the many fishing and pleasure boats tugging at their moorings. The crew of a fishing boat sold their catch on the quayside, weighing fish in handheld scales, watched by a group of tourists. Behind her, palm trees, the bell tower and dome of the church, two of the landmarks her father had used to guide them home from the sea.

Hot from her walk, Popi was tempted to take a seat in one of the many cafes that lined the seafront. She knew if she sat down she might never start ticking items off her list. She walked along the path which skirted the sea, leading from the square in the direction of the narrow causeway out to the bridge across the canal. Smiling, she politely rejected the advances of the street waiters, each determined she would eat in their taverna.

Although she had walked here many times before, the sea still had the capacity to distract her. Within that timeless view lay infinite pictures painted by changes in the light, winds, weather, time and season. Lost in thoughts, her appetite for shopping had all but disappeared by the time the path joined the main road. Popi window-shopped as she walked back towards the harbour. Little she saw enticed her to buy, until she saw a highly-glazed, bright orange smiling sun for sale. Something about it made her smile and she had to get it. Leaving the shop with her carefully wrapped sun and a set of blue-and-white salt and pepper shakers, Popi realised she was perhaps in the wrong place and state of mind to shop for essentials. She would go to Agios Nikolaos in a few days to concentrate on her list. She stopped off at the Post Office. The only letter for her there was the acceptance of her resignation from the university.

She returned to the path beside the sea, this time taking up the offer of a table right on the waterfront. Despite her breakfast, the walk and the sea air had given her an appetite. As she sat eating the water seemed to be calling her. '*Avrio*. Tomorrow', she told herself. 'Tomorrow my boat will be at sea.'

Walking back up the donkey track to the village, Popi questioned the wisdom of having eaten lunch and the journey was slow. As she walked through the village, she was greeted by the same elderly people, still chatting in their seats outside the taverna. She let herself into the house and walked out onto the terrace. From the olive grove she could hear a clanking sound. She rounded the corner of the house to see her uncle and boyfriend feeding metres of chain into the anchor locker at the bow of the caique.

Already they had connected up the radio, GPS, echo sounder and other paraphernalia. Bright orange lifebuoys had been mounted on the stanchions and blue fenders stashed in the cockpit lockers.

'We're almost ready to take to the water,' said Spyros, smiling. 'We even bought a fish finder. You know how I can't resist a gadget, and I'm sure you'll find it useful.'

Reaching in her bag, Popi pulled out the bubble-wrapped ceramic sun and handed the package to Costas. Unwrapping the parcel he grinned back at the orange smiling face before climbing the stairs to the cockpit and mounting it on the bulkhead.

137

Although they had agreed to meet at 8 o'clock the next morning, by half-past seven Popi and Costas found themselves anxiously waiting in the olive grove, to be quickly joined by Yiannis, two of his mechanics and Spyros. Popi's uncle looked back on the day he had stopped his brother-in-law from setting fire to the frame of the boat. It was poignant to recall how they had hauled it up the hill to where it now stood in its completed glory.

The finished craft was a lot heavier than the frame had been. The men had painstakingly planned how to get the caique loaded by hoisting the bow and sliding the trailer underneath then using the mechanical winch on Spyros' four-by-four to slide it forward into position. With the hull secured by straps, Costas climbed into the cockpit, then Spyros manoeuvred his truck out of the olive grove onto the mountain road.

Pulling out in front of the caique, Yiannis took his position at the front of the convoy and Thea was joined by Popi bringing up the rear. Daunted by the task ahead, Popi's anxiety abated as her uncle slowly but confidently navigated the tight bends. Several motorbikes overtook the vehicles and the workers on the local refuse lorry joyfully waved and hooted their horn as they fell into line behind. All waited patiently as a flock of sheep was driven across the road, the shepherd raising his crook in greeting.

When they entered Elounda, business owners came out of their shops and tavernas to cheer them on, and Popi noticed they had unofficially cordoned off the road to stop traffic meeting them on their descent. The warmth with which they were greeted brought a tear to Popi's eye as the esteem in which her father was held suddenly hit her. If she needed any more confirmation of how he had been loved by his community, this was it.

Navigating the roundabout on the waterfront they headed along the coast road. A group of locals followed at walking pace as the caique made its way out of the town. Reaching the slipway which ran across the sands near where her father's boatyard had stood, Spyros confidently reversed the trailer toward the water. Costas threw down a bowline to Yiannis before retreating to the cockpit. As the boat was inched into the sea, Costas released the straps and when it reached a depth where the boat could float, *Katerina* was set free with a push from Yiannis who was standing waist deep in the water. The small crowd who had gathered to watch clapped as the caique took to the bay, their cheers drowned out as Costas turned the ignition, the engine responding first time.

With the motor in neutral, Costas walked forward to retrieve the bowline, coiling it on the foredeck before returning to the tiller and picking up a mooring buoy. Thea put an arm around her niece; she could see how the relief of seeing her dream come true had made the young woman emotional. The boat that now graced the waters of the bay stood as a link to the past, her lost father, her mother and her future happiness. Popi looked up to see Costas standing on the bow waving his t-shirt before diving into the water and swimming ashore. Dripping wet he embraced her, the salt-water mingling with her tears of joy.

'*Efharisto*. Thank you,' whispered Popi.

Well-wishers were still turning up to congratulate Popi, Costas and Spyros on what they had achieved. Not only was the caique a thing of beauty, but for many it stood as a triumph against all the adversity so many had suffered in recent years. Although the day was still young, a plastic container of raki and some glasses had found its way to the waterfront and Spyros proposed a toast.

'To Manolis, Popi, Costas, Katerina and this superb caique named after her.'

Chapter 8

'YOU FINALLY FINISHED my boat then.'

Turning, the group saw a dishevelled fat man, his red face contorted and dripping with perspiration, stumbling towards them from the Old Boatyard taverna, which now stood on the waterfront where Manolis once ran his business.

Spyros was the first to react, turning to head off the man, followed by Yiannis. Costas remained rooted to the spot.

'Give it up, Christos.' Spyros stood in front of the man, who was clearly drunk, despite the early hour. 'There's nothing of interest to you here.'

'I want my share of the boat.' Spyros held his ground. 'You villagers have taken everything from me. Spreading rumours so no one will use my taverna. That boatbuilder would have gone broke anyway. Why am I to blame if he was stupid?'

A gold medallion glistened beneath the fat man's soiled shirt and Spyros stepped forward and made a grab for it. Yiannis caught his friend's arm just in time.

'You are owed nothing, and if I hear mention of it again I will repay you in a way we should have all those years ago,' said Yiannis. The burly garage owner let go of his friend and stepped around him to confront Christos.

Popi was unsure of what was going on, but she did know that the mood of the morning had turned as sour as the stink of sweat coming from the angry, drunk man. Was he talking about her father, and how could anyone have a claim to her caique?

'I paid a deposit when I commissioned the boat, I am owed my…' Dodging around Yiannis, Spyros launched himself at the man before he could finish, wrestling him to the ground, only to be pulled off him by his friend.

'Are you going to stand there and let them get away with this?' The drunk man demanded of Costas, whose gaze was fixed on the ground as everyone turned towards him.

The young boatbuilder wanted the silence to swallow him. Why had he not realised his happiness could not last? This man had destroyed his future before. Now it was happening again. All of a sudden, he knew he had to get away.

'They can do what they like, uncle.'

142

Costas turned to face Popi. He opened his mouth, but no words came and in that moment of hesitation he knew that he was lost.

'Popi.' Costas reached out a hand. 'I didn't know.'

The moment the words left the young man's lips, Thea reached for her niece's hand. Popi's glance stopped Costas in his tracks. She hadn't heard the full story, but she could sense that the fat man pulling himself off the sand had played a part in her father's demise, the loss of his business, the subsequent breakup of her parents' marriage, her having to leave the country of her birth. And he was Costas' uncle! What part had he had to play in the ruination of her father?

Opening his mouth as if to speak, Christos was silenced by a look from Spyros that penetrated even his addled mind.

'If you ever say anything to harm anyone in my family again, I will come for you. Believe me, it will not just be your pocket that will be hurting.' Spyros pushed Christos back on the sand. He rose and scuttled off in the direction of his taverna.

Popi had seen and heard enough. One look from her stopped Costas from following as she turned and walked away to Thea's car. For a moment Costas watched her go. How had he even dared to hope that things might turn out well for him? Looking down, he slowly made his escape in the direction of Elounda.

143

Spyros quietly thanked Yiannis and his assistant, who retreated to their truck. Left alone on the beach, he stared out across the water to where the caqiue lay on her mooring, turning her bow this way and that as the lightest of zephyrs danced across the waters. They were so close to finishing the vessel and starting the business. Costas had done a magnificent job, there was no doubt that the boat was splendid. He knew that the gift Manolis had left to his daughter had done so much to heal the sadness of her past and to secure her a future. As he gazed across the sapphire bay was dappled with glints of silver as the sun picked out the tiny peaks of ripples blown towards the distant canal and out to the sunken city beyond.

Already their caique looked as though it belonged here. He had seen how happy it had made his niece. Since they had employed Costas, he had grown to like him. He knew that by finishing the boat the young man had hoped to assuage the guilt he felt about his uncle's dealings with Manolis. But it was clear to him that Costas had not known of his uncle's intentions all those years ago. If back then Christos had managed to destroy the future for his brother-in-law's family, Spyros was determined he would not let him ruin their lives again.

Leaving his truck and trailer parked in the shade of a tamarisk tree, he walked back along the coast road to Elounda. As he passed the Old Boatyard taverna, he felt the gaze of a pair of eyes drilling into his back. Reaching the town, it didn't take him long to find Costas sitting inside a kafenio by the harbour, staring into a glass of beer.

'May I join you?' Spyros approached the table. Looking up Costas signalled for him to sit.

'I should have known better.' Almost immediately Costas opened up. 'I knew things would end up like this. My uncle always finds a way to ruin my life. Popi will never forgive me, and who can blame her now she knows that it was Christos who wrecked her father's business and marriage and drove her out of her home?'

'Just give her some time,' reassured Spyros, turning to order a beer from the barman.

'Popi is upset now, but I know she has feelings for you. She is not stupid. She has seen the love you have put into finishing the boat. She will come round. I will talk to her and try and persuade her not to let this ruin her future. We just need to give her some days to calm down first.'

'I should have told her the truth.' Costas took a deep swallow from his glass. 'I was too scared that I would lose her and she would not let me build the caique.'

Spyros couldn't help but admit to himself that Costas was right. Maybe he should have trusted his first instincts. Had he been too intent to get the business going and see his niece's future back home on Crete secured? If Popi had known how Christos had intentionally manipulated her father to make him bankrupt so he could buy the lease on the land for his taverna, she would never have considered Costas for the work. And what would his niece think when she realised he had kept the past a secret from her?

As the morning wore into lunchtime and afternoon, Spyros let the young man unburden himself of the story of his past. He leant a sympathetic ear and listened in silence as Costas told him how he had found himself in the custody of his father's brother, a man he had not previously known, following the death of his mother from cancer and his father's subsequent breakdown. Since that day when he was 11-years-old, he had never seen his father again and he learned that he had died in an asylum near Athens.

Costas' uncle had little time for his new charge. Grieving for the loss of his parents the boy found it hard to settle into school in the northern port city of Thessaloniki where his uncle lived. Christos was rarely at home, always out wheeling and dealing. Left to his own devices, the young lad left school without any qualifications.

Their move to Crete had been sudden, his uncle packing and leaving their home on the mainland overnight, driving south to catch the ferry the following evening from Piraeus to Heraklion. If their departure from Thessaloniki had been abrupt, for Costas it marked the start of a more settled time in his life. His uncle had managed to secure him an apprenticeship with the boatbuilder, Manolis. Responding to the kindness shown towards him, Costas quickly displayed an aptitude for his craft. Although he realised times were hard for Manolis, his boss always managed to find enough work to get by and keep them both busy. When his uncle decided to commission a caique from Manolis, Costas had thought his future was secure. He had never seen his employer so happy as they embarked on laying down the frame for the craft.

Some months later, his world had come crashing down when Manolis told his apprentice he would have to let him go as he was having to close the business. The boatbuilder had spared the boy's feelings and had not explained his uncle's involvement in his demise. But it was not long before rumours of the truth behind his guardian's chicanery reached his ears. With nowhere to go and with a misplaced family loyalty towards his uncle, he stayed on in the home they shared as the whole unscrupulous business unfolded. Christos seemed unconcerned that he was hated by the locals but, for the unemployed Costas to whom Manolis had been so kind, it was purgatory.

Using the excuse of being unable to find work locally, the young boatbuilder rented a cheap room in Agios Nikolaos and touted his skills around the marina. At first he lived from hand-to-mouth, but at least he had escaped the acrimony his association with his uncle had heaped on him. In the early days he would return to his uncle's for a meal on his day off, but as time went on these visits became less regular and the two grew apart. Christos showed little interest in his nephew's wellbeing and Costas felt pleased when he did not have to visit him.

Meanwhile, his uncle's business was struggling to establish itself. None of the locals would use the taverna. Many actively warned tourists off going there too, and as taxes increased as the recession bit deeper, Christos was forced to dig into his own pockets to keep it going. But he was a stubborn man, and despite all the signs that the business was a failure, in the face of everything he kept it open. None of the local chefs or waiters would work there, and he had to rely on recruiting staff who had not heard of his dirty dealings, and when these outsiders got to hear about what their boss had done, they soon left.

With little to do and stressed by his inability to make the taverna pay, Christos had taken to drink. Locals had grown used to seeing him sitting alone in the taverna, a bottle his only company. Some still smiled at his demise as they walked past. Others had to remind themselves what had brought the businessman to this point before they banished any scintilla of sympathy which might have entered into their hearts.

Living in Agios Nikolaos, Costas had managed to distance himself from the bad feelings towards his uncle. Although things were easier for him there, he missed the sense of belonging he had felt when working for Manolis. As an apprentice, for the first time since he had lost his parents he had been aware of a purpose in his life. His boss had treated him as part of his family and had believed in him. He loved working with wood, creating and maintaining the boats using skills which had been passed down through generations of boatbuilders. Now, although he had not been part of his uncle's duplicity, he found it impossible to shake the guilt his relationship with Christos heaped upon him.

Working on the plastic boats in the marina paid the bills; it left him feeling unfulfilled, but at least the numbness had protected him from the hurt he now felt. Working on the caique, he had felt reborn and in his relationship with Popi he had found a love he could never have imagined. Now it had all come to this. She would never forgive him, and who could blame her?

'Tomorrow I suggest you start work rigging the mast and wiring in the last of the navigation lights.' Spyros voice penetrated the fog of Costas' self-pity. Surely, thought Costas, he did not want him to continue working on the boat after all that had happened?

'We need to get the boat fully seaworthy so Popi can start her tours. Running away will sort nothing. Perhaps if you continue to

149

help with the boat she will come round to realising you had nothing to do with your uncle's treatment of her dad.'

Perhaps Spyros was right. He had been running away for much of his young life. It was worth fighting for the woman and the life he loved.

'If I am to work tomorrow, I should go home and get some sleep.' Costas rose unsteadily to his feet.

'You can stay with us. You're in no state to drive, and your scooter is in the village.' Spyros steadied the young man with an arm as he led him out into the sunlight.

*

Popi had run out of tears as she rose from her bed. Exhausted from crying, a siesta had proved a welcome sanctuary. Out on the terrace, she watched the sun dropping down towards the mountains, infusing the sky with a red wash before illuminating it in orange. She could not deny herself its beauty but struggled to reconcile it with how wretched she felt inside. It was clear to her now why Costas had at first seemed reluctant to work on the boat. And Spyros, he had been doubtful too. He must have known about Christos and that he was Costas' uncle all along.

Below her the bay was turning inky black. Lights came on one by one reflected in the water and echoed by the stars in the darkening sky. How amidst so much beauty could she feel so much pain? She was sure after what she now saw as Costas' betrayal that she felt nothing for him, but still something wrenched at her heart. She had loved her time back here on the island and for the first time since she was a child had felt her life was rooted. Now she was conflicted about the future. The allure of her surroundings stood at odds with her emotions, making it impossible to think. Disconcerted she returned to her bed, but sleep would not come. The sheets held the smell of her lover whilst her head could not grasp her thoughts. Sometime not long before dawn, sleep took her.

She did not hear the sound of Costas' scooter as he set off down the hill to restart work on the boat, but was awoken by a knock on the door from her uncle. Drunk from her troubled sleep, Popi reached deep into herself to recollect the previous day. Shouldn't she be angry with her uncle?

'I'm sorry, Popi.' Stepping over the threshold, Spyros hugged his niece. 'I should have told you, but you seemed so happy.'

The embrace disarmed her but she again felt an overwhelming sadness.

'You get dressed, and I'll make the coffee.' Spyros stepped towards the kitchen.

If her short sleep had taken the edge off her anger, it had done little to resolve the way Popi felt about her future. As they sat drinking coffee on the terrace, she knew in her heart that her uncle

151

was right when he told her it would be foolish to throw away her dream of staying on Crete now that the boat was finished. But there was something pulling her towards the security of her mother's love and her life in England. Her uncle said that what had happened in the past should not be allowed to affect her life yet again. Should she stay strong and remain?

Spyros could see that Popi needed time to think things through. He hoped that over the following days she would put things into perspective. His intuition told him to give her the space she needed to work things out for herself.

*

Costas was as good as his word. Each day he would swim out to the caique before bringing her alongside the small jetty, where he would work tying and wiring the rigging and screwing and fixing the final fittings required to make *Katerina* seaworthy. Spyros would pop down to the quay most days to monitor the young man's progress but kept clear of Popi, giving her time to come to terms with her feelings.

After four days, Costas had readied the caique for the first of its sea trials and Spyros was happy to join the boatbuilder on board. He had secured a berth alongside his own boat in the harbour, and after a few hours out at sea they planned to return to the town quay in readiness for future trials. Spyros was passionate about his own caique, but within moments of being aboard he could see that the new boat was just as perfect. Leaving the jetty behind, Costas passed the tiller over to Spyros, who nudged the throttle forward, relishing how the boat's broad beam comfortably rode the swell. It was responsive to the helm without being pushed off course by gusts of wind or the wash from other boats.

Being at sea calmed the disquiet Costas felt over his break-up with Popi. He had not seen her since that day she had walked away from him on the beach. He appreciated Spyros' support, knowing that if all else was lost, he was at least still welcome in the community. At sea he was able to clear his mind. Perhaps in time Popi would come round and realise that he had had nothing to do with his uncle's plan.

For Popi, the first days since her discovery of Christos' fateful double-crossing of her father had seen her in a deep well of despondency. She tried to tell herself that she was better off without Costas but, if that were the case, why did she feel their separation so keenly? As the days passed the whirlwind of her anger began to blow itself out and, as she grew calmer, she allowed herself to think about the future.

After another restless night of fitful sleep, Popi awoke to find the rage had abated. Despite everything that had happened, she could not remember feeling so at one with the spirit of a place as she

153

did on the island. She still had the house in the village, her boat on the bay and her plans for the business. All these things had been made possible by her father. If she threw all these away it would be a further betrayal of her dad. After the break-up of his marriage, he had somehow found the strength to rebuild his life, fighting all the odds to win some security for the daughter he would never see again. The boat was a talisman that would sail her through any choppy waters that lay ahead. And Costas had made this happen.

It had been five days since they had floated *Katerina* and her dreams had been sunk. Sitting on the terrace, she allowed herself for the first time in days to relax. The cacophony of cicadas was unable to compete with the lullaby of distant goat bells and the warm blanket the sun pulled over her as she succumbed to sleep.

Opening her eyes, she could see the bay glistening like a jewel in the distance, a boat drawing a fine filigree of silver out over its sapphire surface. Looking up at the mountains, the sun had not long reached its zenith, infusing the air with a rich bouquet of wild herbs. Her eye returned to the caique heading up Korfos towards Elounda; something in it held her gaze. As the dusts of sleep blew away, Popi was sure she recognised the vessel. She could just make out two people standing in the cockpit and her instinct confirmed what her eyes could not clearly see.

It was hard to imagine a view more perfect. The boat looked as though it had been made to be in this place at this peerless moment. As it moved towards the little harbour, Popi felt the caique reel her in the same direction. Her mind was made up; she was meant to be here in the village where she was born. The caique was now as much a part of her life as it was part of the living, breathing bay below. And maybe she was meant to be with Costas. It had been unkind of her to walk away without allowing him any chance to explain himself. He had helped her to realise the dream of finishing the boat, supported her and shown her love and she had treated him like this. Maybe it was not too late.

Popi slipped on her shoes, grabbed her bag and a hat before closing the front door behind her and setting off down through the lanes to the donkey track. Distracted and nervous about seeing Costas again, she had to remind herself to keep looking down so as not to trip on the uneven stones. A dog dragged her from her thoughts, barking as he reached the end of his chain, his front legs up on the wall of the land he was protecting. She continued walking, relieved that the guard dog was tethered.

In the village the day-to-day shops had already closed for siesta although those catering for tourists remained open in the hope of afternoon trade. An old lady dressed in her widow's weeds snoozed on a chair in the shade of a tree outside the church. The roads were quiet as Popi crossed the car park to the harbour-front. There alongside her uncle's boat was her caique. She thought how they looked the finest boats in the harbour, and her father had had a hand in creating both. She felt her heart swell with pride at the thought, and also remembered the role Costas had in finishing the newer vessel.

Aboard *Katerina* the lines had all been neatly coiled, the companionway hatch padlocked and a sun canopy rigged over the boom to protect the varnish work in the cockpit. Popi smiled to herself as a tourist stopped to take a picture of the two boats side by side on the quay. She had hoped to catch Costas and her uncle before they left the caique but maybe they had stopped for a drink at one of the harbourside cafes. It would not take her long to see if they were there, perhaps she could join them.

Turning her eyes from the water, almost immediately she spotted Spyros leaving a cafe and striding out along the road towards Plaka. She raised a hand to wave and mouthed a silent greeting, but he did not look up. Perhaps Costas was still there? Her spirits high, she determined to go and look. She wanted to see him, to apologise for walking away and to try and build a bridge towards a new future together. A delivery lorry stopping to unload crates of drink blocked her way. Popi walked behind the vehicle, knowing any hesitation might break her resolve.

Safely on the other side of the road she stopped for a moment to check her smile before stepping through the open door of the cafe. The air-conditioned cool inside was welcoming and Popi blinked to adjust her eyes as she came in out of the sunlight. At first she could not see Costas; then her eye caught the back of his head at a table in the corner of the room. Just as Popi was about to approach she was pulled up short by the realisation that he was not alone. A bright red sun hat was the first thing she saw of his companion, then beneath the striking headwear she made out the even more striking face of a young woman, who appeared to be hanging on Costas' every word. Even from behind, Popi could tell from the movement of his hands that her former lover was lost in animated conversation.

The scorching heat of the afternoon sun did not match the burning in her cheeks as she stepped back outside. Embarrassed she quickly walked away not wanting to be seen. She held back her tears until she reached the bottom of the donkey track and then the floodgates opened. A welter of thoughts flooded her mind. How could he have moved on from her so quickly? Why had she been so stupid and walked away from the man she loved in the first place? Why had she thought that she could ever be happy?

Distraught, and ashamed that anyone should see her, she avoided the village streets. Where the track crossed the mountain road she followed it, entering the olive grove through the gap in the wall through which less than a week before they had hauled the caique. She walked past the still flattened, parched grass where the boat had once stood. It would have been better to have left it there and spared herself the heartache which her foolish dreams had led her to.

Inside the house she rinsed her face under the cold tap before pouring herself a glass of water. Interrupted by a knock on the door, she stood still. She could not be seen in this state and wanted to be alone with her thoughts. Popi thought her breathing was so loud it would penetrate even the thick stone walls of the house. Through the closed shutters she heard the voices of Spyros and Thea, and then their footsteps walking down the lane.

How dare her uncle come to find her? He knew that Costas was in the cafe with the woman in the hat. He had been out on the boat with Costas all day too. Why had he not told her about Costas' uncle in the first place? She had been mad to listen to him and think that she could make a future for herself back here. Having burned her boats back in England by resigning, she felt trapped. There was nobody here that she could trust.

Popi had no appetite to eat or to go out. She sought the comfort of her bed but found it difficult to rest. She kept going over and over the events of the short time she had been back on Crete. Occasionally a picture of *Katerina* sailing across the bay flashed through her mind but was all too soon washed away by thoughts of her betrayal by Costas and her uncle. If only she could hold onto the image of her beautiful boat, perhaps it would help her find some peace and perspective. As evening turned to night, Popi's relentless thoughts would not let her sleep. As dawn began to filter through the shutters of her room, it cast no light on her darkest thoughts.

Lying in bed was torture, her brain spinning like the sails of a windmill in a storm. Distractedly she washed and dressed and stepped out into the half light of the new day, made her way to the mountain road and mounted the scooter her father had left her. In Elounda, as the shutters on the cafes came up, she stopped for a coffee but it couldn't clear the fog in her head. On auto pilot, Popi headed out of town, her dark hair blowing out behind her and the breeze drying the moisture from her eyes as she climbed. Concentrating on the winding road ahead, she realised where she was heading.

At the top of the hill before the road headed inland to the mountains, she stopped. Turning off the engine, the silence was palpable. She walked towards the cliff edge and stared over the abyss. Below her was Turtle Beach. She took a step back; she did not trust herself as the memories flooded her troubled mind. The beach below had been the secret place she shared with her dad all those years ago. It had been there that he had told her of the breakdown of the marriage and how she was leaving for England. It was to this very spot that she had come to seek solace on the day her father was buried, and to the cove below that she had taken Costas just a few months ago.

Calmer now, she sat close to the cliff edge and let the beauty which lay beneath her feet soothe the swell of her gushing thoughts. The warmth of the rising sun on her face, she stared out at the Aegean, spread out to where it met the sky. Sitting here gave her a perspective which calmed the fury which had been raging inside her. Somehow she would work things out and find a way to stay.

Out to sea a boat etched a white line as it moved tentatively across the immaculate blue canvas. Below, the sands of the little cove were golden, not yet bleached to white by the full attentions of the sun. Popi remembered her father telling her about the turtles which hatched beneath the sands, emerging only at night to make their perilous journey down the beach into the sea. She smiled at the memory and a shaft of light shone through her sorrow.

Looking seawards, she saw the boat motoring closer inshore. How she wished she was out there now, surrounded by the healing waters of the ocean. Why didn't she go out? After all, the caique was hers, and if it was out on sea trials she had the keys to her uncle's boat which he had said she could use any time.

As she stood, something about the lone caique caught her eye. Popi was sure she recognised the lines and the way the hull rode the waves. As the boat came closer to the shore it was unmistakable. It was her boat, heading towards Turtle Beach with Costas at the tiller. How dare he take her boat out to her secret place? All the comfort she had found in the previous moments was instantly dashed on the rocks of her former lover's betrayal. If she had felt distraught before, now all she felt was anger. Fixedly staring as *Katerina* held a course towards the cove, her anger turned to rage as she saw a red hat emerge into the cockpit from the cabin below.

Chapter 9

POPI DID NOT know what had come over her. She was devoid of reason and just let the anger guide her. She had never felt so betrayed in her life. The man she had felt sure she had a future with had taken another woman to her secret place. The secret place she had shared with her father. He had gone there on her boat, the boat named after her mother.

It was not just a betrayal of herself but of her whole family. She felt guilty for ever having revealed the whereabouts of Turtle Beach to Costas. The anger grew as she descended the mountain, throwing the scooter around the hairpin bends.

Skidding to a halt beside her uncle's boat she leaped aboard, not bothering to close the gap by hauling on the mooring line. Working purely on intuition, she prepared the caique for sea. She would not let Costas get away with this. Popi was determined to confront him at the very moment of his betrayal. To let him know they were finished, that he was not welcome on her boat or on her secret beach. She would show the woman in the red hat what an untrustworthy bastard she was getting involved with. She was welcome to him. Why, oh why had she not trusted her own instincts when the truth about Costas and his uncle had been revealed the day they launched the boat?

Untying the bow line, she returned to the cockpit and dropped the rope from the mooring buoy astern. With the tiller amidships she engaged reverse and took the caique into the pool of the harbour before pushing the gear lever forwards and setting a course for Spinalonga. At sea her anger turned from red to white; no longer burning rage but a cold determination. She felt herself shiver as a slight onshore breeze brushed her warm cheek. Looking around she slowed the boat and lifted the cockpit locker to take out a waterproof jacket.

As she reached the narrow channel between the island and Kalidon, Popi felt the boat beneath her twitch as the wind funnelling through the gap hit the topsides. The white caps on the shallow water gave notice of the rising wind blowing in off the sea. Popi steered the boat north of the island into the wider, deep-water channel. Here the waves were not breaking but rolled beneath the sturdy hull which comfortably fell in with their relentless rhythm.

Turning to hug the coast, the swell hit the caique broadside and Popi instinctively worked the helm, turning the bow into the peaks as they struck.

Both she and the caique relished the conditions. She loved the feel of spray on her face and the wind blowing her hair and, as the waves grew and the breeze increased, her concentration heightened. She slid back the companionway hatch to keep things dry below and glanced at the compass. Out to sea the sky had grown dark, the rain-laden skies mingling with the leaden waters. A flash of lightning for an instant restored that defining line as a rumble of thunder rode in on the wind.

Looking along the shoreline, she could see columns of spray as waves broke on the cliffs which tumbled into the sea. Popi surveyed the mountainside for the glint of white which would signal the small chapel and guide her towards the cove. A fork of lightning illuminated the mountainside, picking out the lonely church, in that instant she looked at the compass and mentally set a course. The clash of thunder which closely followed announced the full potency of the storm was almost upon her. Absorbed in navigating the caique, Popi had put to the back of her mind the looming encounter with Costas. Somehow as the storm increased in intensity, her anger had abated. Now she wondered how she was going to handle their impending confrontation. She was not concerned for his safety; he was as experienced as she was aboard a boat and Popi was sure that the caique he had built would comfortably withstand these testing conditions.

Popi let go of these considerations as she steered towards the mouth of the bay. With the wind coming in from the sea the entrance to the cove would be on a lee shore so she would need to keep her wits about her. Spotting the gap between the two rocky headlands she swung the tiller over and felt the swell pick the caique up by its broad beam and carry it towards the entrance to the cove. She could tell by the way the sea rolled straight through the narrow channel, the waves only breaking on the rocky arms which formed the opening, that shelter inside the bay would be limited. Checking her course on the compass one last time she looked up. The entrance was now in clear sight and she could navigate by eye.

Although these were nervous moments, Popi relished the rush of adrenaline and had confidence in her own ability. As she approached the mouth of the cove a large wave lifted the stern of the caique. Instinctively, Popi gripped the tiller more firmly, surfing the boat between the headlands and prepared to change course to find a sheltered spot to drop anchor.

As the wave dropped her into its trough she was in. She looked around as the next peak lifted the hull again.

'What the…!'

Popi shrieked, slamming the helm over. She took the risk of the next wave catching her broadside on. Pushing the throttle hard forward, she hoped the boat would respond quickly. It did not let her down, the aft quarter just missing the bow of *Katerina*. Slowing her breathing she could see the plight of the other caique. On the foredeck, Costas was struggling with the windlass. His anchor must have snagged. He had motored the boat above the jammed hook to try and use the force of the waves to free it, but this left him desperately exposed as the waves lifted the bow before slamming it down into the trough. It was no good; he would have to ditch the anchor chain. Carefully Costas made his way aft, giving instructions to his companion who clutched the helm. He went below; Popi realised he must be disconnecting the chain from its fixing. Re-emerging with a knife, Costas ran forward. Reaching the bow, he pulled the remaining chain from the locker.

He stooped to unfasten the chain from the cleat, before unsheathing his knife to cut through the rope which took the weight off the winch. The large roller broke over the bow just as he stooped, slamming his head on a stanchion as it washed him overboard. At the helm, the woman stood frozen as panic gripped her. *Katerina* was still at anchor, held by the rope strop that remained uncut.

In calmer water, Popi swung the caique around in an arc heading towards the beach before steering back out towards the stern of the other boat. In an instant she released a lifebuoy from the guardrail. As the surf rolled in, at slow speed the boat pitched wildly. On the peak of a wave she caught a glimpse of a yellow life vest in the water and heaved the line. The buoy landed just a few feet from Costas, but was he conscious and did he have the strength to make it even that far?

Keeping her eye on the floating body she reached for the lifebuoy on the other side of the cockpit. She saw Costas raise an arm and with a monumental effort take the two stokes it needed to reach the buoy in the water. Popi felt her spirits lift for a moment. She took turns around a winch and heaved. Slowly she dragged the motionless body of Costas towards the boat. She needed to keep the engine running to stop the boat from being washed onto the beach. She dropped a boarding ladder from the bow so Costas would not come near the turning propeller, hoping upon hope he would have the strength to climb aboard. Lying on the foredeck she reached an arm down and Costas grabbed it. Somehow, with Popi's help, he found enough strength to climb aboard.

Blood was smeared over his face. The chill of the wind on his damp body was making him shake. Grabbing blankets and the first aid kit from below, Popi wrapped him up and made him as comfortable as she could in the cockpit before cleaning the wound on his forehead. The gash was deep, but with a heavily strapped

167

dressing she managed to stem the bleeding. She knew he needed to go to hospital to get the wound stitched and be checked over.

Manoeuvring the caique close to *Katerina*, Popi shouted to the frightened woman in the cockpit. Before asking her if she felt OK to follow her and helm the boat home, she knew the answer. There was no way Popi could risk leaving *Katerina* on a snagged anchor, now held only by a rope strop. She would need to take the vessel in tow.

The woman seemed relieved that Popi had taken control of the situation. Shouting instructions from her uncle's caique, Popi threw a line aboard *Katerina*, instructing the frightened woman to carefully walk it forward and secure it around the stempost, and then to cut free the rope strop and ditch the anchor.

Popi felt the weight of *Katerina* on the towline and shifted the throttle forward to take up the strain as the woman aboard the stricken caique edged her way aft to safety of the cockpit. Popi looked back; she no longer felt any anger towards Costas' friend as she gripped hard on the tiller of the boat in tow. She could sense the tension on the woman's face as she concentrated to hold *Katerina* on a steady course. Out of the wind, Costas had stopped shivering and blood was no longer seeping through his dressing but Popi was concerned that he was drowsy and gave a running commentary about her progress to try and keep him engaged.

With her anger exhausted, Popi reassured herself that she had been right to follow her caique out to sea, if she had not been there, the outcome would have been tragic. As they passed through the narrow entrance to the cove, the breaking waves tossed the boats mercilessly. When Popi reached the crest of a wave, the boat in tow would wrench her back as it pitched into a trough. The rope held firm, and in the open sea the going got easier. Out on the horizon a strip of light separated the sea from the sky. The storm had moved inshore and rumbled around the mountains.

The heavy sea now rolled under the two vessels. Although uncomfortable, Popi felt confident in both boats and her own ability to ride out the storm. Unwilling to leave the helm whilst in such choppy waters, she decided to forgo the radio and reached inside her waterproof to find her mobile phone. There was a signal. She dialled her uncle's number.

As they passed the island of Spinalonga, and headed south through the calmer waters of the bay of Korfos, Popi could see the flashing blue lights of the ambulance Spyros had promised to call waiting by the quayside in Elounda. With *Katerina* still in tow she jockeyed the bow of her uncle's caique to the quay so Spyros could jump aboard and throw a line ashore. In no time her uncle and the paramedics had Costas off the boat. Popi secured her own mooring

169

before winching in the towline and transferring to *Katerina* to slide her into the berth alongside.

Whilst Popi was busying herself with the lines, Costas' friend, carrying a rather bedraggled red hat, gingerly made her way towards the bow. Spyros held out his hand to help her ashore.

'Maria, are you alright?'

Popi looked up to see her uncle put his arm around the young woman's shoulders. In that instant, the feelings of betrayal swamped her again.

'I would be a lot worse if it hadn't been for her.' Maria turned and gestured towards Popi.

It was not the woman's fault. She did not even know who Popi was. It was Costas, now disappearing in the ambulance towards Agios Nikolaos, who she should blame along with her uncle who obviously knew her rival in love. Pretending not to hear, Popi continued to stow away lines and wet weather gear and mount the lifebuoy back on the guardrail before transferring to her own caique and making it shipshape again.

Popi stepped ashore to be greeted by a hug from Maria. 'I can't thank you enough. I don't know what we would have done if you hadn't been there.'

'It really was nothing,' mumbled Popi, rendered unresponsive by her confusion.

'Have you two been introduced?' Spyros looked from one young woman to the other.

Now Spyros was going too far. Maria could see by the look on Popi's face that something made this an inappropriate time for polite introductions.

'Thank you again. I really must get back to my hotel and out of these wet clothes.'

'You're welcome.' Popi managed to force the words from her lips.

'You knew her?' Popi turned to her uncle, her eyes welling up with tears.

In that moment Spyros understood and his heart went out to his niece. He put an arm around her shoulders. 'We need to get you home, warm and dry and have a chat.'

Popi pulled away, but tired and upset let herself be led to her uncle's truck and driven up the mountain to the village.

Seeing the state of Popi, Thea got towels and went to her niece's house to find her dry clothes. Returning, she made hot chocolate which she served with a plate of cinnamon and honey *loukoumades*, the fried dough balls accompanied by warming raki. As she sat on the terrace Popi could hear the occasional grumble of thunder high in the mountains. The dusk sky had cleared and the warmth of the evening sun drying the hillside brought the

171

comforting aroma of herbs and wildflowers. Tiredness had taken the edge off her hunger and as she sat contemplating the events of the day she felt an overwhelming sense of numbness.

Spyros, accompanied by Thea, came outside to join her on the terrace.

'I don't care who Costas sees, uncle.' Spyros was not sure that was true. 'What upset me was he took his new girlfriend to my secret place, in my boat, and it appears you knew all about it.' Popi's resigned tones told her uncle she was too tired to fight.

'His new girlfriend?' said her uncle.

'After what he and his uncle had done to dad, he betrayed me again… And you knew all along!'

'Spyros only did what he thought right Popi.' Thea placed her hand on Popi's. 'And not everything is as it seems. Please give him time to explain.'

As the light faded, Spyros told Popi how Costas and he had met Maria who worked for a sea turtle protection agency and wanted to survey nesting grounds to put in place a conservation plan. As Costas was doing sea trials on Popi's caique, he saw no problem in offering to take her to Turtle Beach.

'So she's not his girlfriend?' Although relieved, Popi was still angry that Costas had revealed her secret place.

'No,' said Spyros emphatically. 'And Popi, Turtle Beach is not a secret. That is just something your dad used to tell you. A father talking to his little girl. It was a white lie, but a gift to cherish, to give you a secret you both could share. Yes, the tourists don't know about it, but Costas did, I do and all of the fishermen know where it is as well as the conservation agencies.'

Popi was not sure how she felt. Costas had not betrayed her, but at the same time she was sad that the childhood secret she had thought she had shared with her dad was not a secret after all. She felt the deflation brought on by that loss of innocence. It was like learning Father Christmas was not real. But she was a fully grown adult. How stupid she had been.

'I believe Costas knew nothing of his uncle's plans all those years ago. It would be unfair to make him guilty by association with a man who had treated him so badly.'

In the light of her uncle's explanation, things looked a lot clearer. After all, Costas had finished the boat for them and there was no doubt that it had been a labour of love. It was she who had walked away from him that day on the beach without giving him a chance to tell her the truth. It was she who had jumped to conclusions about the woman in the red hat.

'I feel terrible, uncle.'

'Don't feel too bad, if you hadn't jumped to the wrong conclusion and gone out to Turtle Beach, things might have turned out a lot worse. Perhaps your father was looking out for both of you.'

As the afternoon wore on Spyros explained to his niece what Costas had told him about his childhood and how he had been treated by Christos. Although Popi was tired, she did not feel like sleeping, particularly until she had found out how Costas was. Her uncle phoned the hospital but could not get through to anyone who could give him any news.

A knock on the door halted the conversation. Thea rose to answer, returning moments later with Costas, his head strapped with a bandage.

Popi couldn't hold back a relieved smile as he walked out onto the terrace.

'I came to say thank you.' Costas hesitated as Popi indicated for him to sit but he remained standing.

'You saved my life.'

'How are you? Should you have driven here?' enquired Popi.

'They put a few stitches in the wound and told me to take it easy for a bit. I came by taxi. Listen, Popi, I need to explain… I'm sorry.' Costas looked down.

'It's me who needs to apologise Costa,' said Popi. 'Please sit down.'

This time a relieved Costas sat and accepted the offer of a coffee from Thea.

'Spyros has told me about Maria, Turtle Beach, your uncle, everything,' said Popi quietly. 'I have been stupid jumping to too many conclusions and after all you have done for me. I'm sorry to have been so selfish.'

'I'd have thought the same.' Costas looked up. 'I should have followed you when you walked away on the beach. I was afraid of what you might think when you discovered Christos was my uncle and what he had done to your dad. That's why I tried to keep it from you.'

'I feel responsible for this, Popi,' interjected Spyros. 'When you suggested Costas to do the work on your caique I was scared to tell you about the past. You seemed so content, and seeing him building the boat and a future for you I got scared that by raking over the coals it would destroy your happiness.'

'Here, I bought you this as a thank you.' Costas handed her a small gift-wrapped package.

'What is it?'

'Open it up.'

Popi tore off the wrapping to reveal a small box. Excitedly she snapped open the lid. Nestled in a bed of blue silk glistened a gold necklace. Popi gently took it from the box. Looking at the pendant she could see it was an exquisite long-haired goddess fashioned out of gold.

'Britomartis. I thought it was appropriate.' Costas said gently.

'It's gorgeous.' Somewhere in Popi's memory she recalled the story of the nymph which her father had told her. Spyros smiled. 'The protector of seafarers.'

'I love it. Thank you, Costa.' Standing, Popi reached across the table and hugged him.

'Can we start again; this time with no secrets?'

'I'd love that. May I take you out tomorrow? We could go up into the mountains if we could take your father's car?'

'Take the truck, I don't need it and it's got four-wheel drive,' Spyros offered.

'I must phone a taxi.' Costas stood to get his mobile from the back pocket of his jeans.

'Don't go, Costa, you can stay at my place tonight.' Popi suppressed a smile.

*

The light creeping around the shutters promised a new start. Popi threw open the windows and a sense of joyful expectancy

176

washed in on the flood of a new day. What a difference the last 24 hours had made. Today they could get away from the village by themselves and talk about the future, a future that a day ago had seemed impossible. Not wanting to waste a minute of their trip out, they were soon on the road. Despite a slight throbbing in his head, Costas insisted on driving and from the passenger seat Popi could see the full glory of the newly-polished bay of Korfos spread out before her.

Leaving Elounda behind they climbed the familiar road towards Lenika, and as they reached the summit, the view of Agios Nikolaos and the bay of Mirabello unfolded. A huge cruise ship was tethered to the quay, as a lone fishing boat drew its wake across the approaches to the harbour.

As the road dropped down towards Agios Nikolaos they left the sea behind, bypassing the town. At Kalo Chorio they turned inland, the road almost instantly narrowing as it snaked its way into the hills. Already Popi could feel a cooling of the air as they climbed higher. Looking down from the road, ravines and gorges fell away spectacularly and the regular occurrence of tiny shrines stood as a reminder to the dangers of these roads.

Little could shake Popi from her sense of wellbeing as Costas confidently swung the truck around the switchback bends. Here the landscape changed. It was unlike anything Popi had seen before in

Crete. At a village called Anatoli they took another road, wending their way through a wooded landscape. Costas told her they were near the heart of the Dikti range of mountains and this was a protected forest of Calabrian pine trees, harvested by bees to make some of the most delicious honey on the island.

Around the small villages farmers grew vines, fruit trees and vegetables. On a narrow track Costas brought the truck to a halt, performing a U-turn on the precarious road before parking.

'We are here,' he announced opening the door.

When Popi stepped out of the vehicle, all she could hear was the tinkling of water running down the hills. She felt as though she was at the very heart of the woodland. Everywhere was so green.

'This has always been my favourite place to come when I have needed to get away. I hope you will find it worth the journey.'

Taking Popi by the hand he led her towards a roadside fountain which pooled into a stream. Some steps led up to a glade shaded by trees. Beneath a waterfall which fell from the mountainside a small stone chapel stood, around which the tables and chairs of an outdoor taverna were spread. In the stream which ran through it, watermelons sat cooling in the waters, and in the shade of the hillside cauldrons of food bubbled on open fires.

'This is the chapel and taverna of Agia Paraskevi. Here, look inside the church.' Costas led Popi through the narrow doorway into the darkness. A few flickering candles illuminated the icons and an array of silver and tin tama hanging from ribbons as votive offerings to the saint.

Stepping back outside into the light, they were welcomed by the taverna owner. Showing them the dishes he already had cooking, he talked them through the rest of the menu. Offering to cook them a selection of mezzes and meats he was proud to tell them all the ingredients came from the land nearby.

Small plates of beans, dakos, mountain greens and eggs, local cheese, salads, goat, chicken and lamb were brought, along with carafes of water and dry white wine to their table. Between serving locals and cooking, the owner joined them, talking with enthusiasm about what Popi thought was the best food she had ever tasted.

As lunchtime drifted into afternoon, the couple talked about their pasts. Hearing about Costas' tragic childhood and how he had been neglected by his uncle, Popi felt a sense of guilt for thinking he could have been involved in her father's demise. For his part, Costas was trying to throw off the shame he felt by his association with Christos. Each of them was convinced of one thing. Now they had learned the truth, they never wanted to let each other go again.

On a nearby table an elderly customer was encouraged to play lyra, shaking off the years as he drew his bow across the strings. Somehow his playing reached deep into Popi's soul, bringing back memories from her childhood of nights spent with her father and mother at family celebrations. Hearing the music somehow anchored her to the island on which she had been born. It resonated with the mountains, forests, plains and sea and as the music soared and swooped, in that moment she could not imagine her life being anywhere else on earth.

Costas loved this place. In the dark days after he had lost his job, he had often taken the long drive up to the taverna. It was his escape. Here he felt strong, that he belonged and was not being judged for the actions of his uncle. Sometimes he would dance, losing himself in the magical music which momentarily washed away his troubles.

Could his life get any better than this? As the lyra player wound up the tempo, the music spoke to him. This was his life and he had to grasp it now. He knew what he had to do. Turning to Popi, he opened his mouth. As he did, her lips echoed his own words.

'Marry me.' The proposals in unison, the couple's acceptance of each other also resounded as one. Offering a hand, Costas led Popi to a space between the tables. Instinctively the lyra player drew out a slow, haunting melody, accompanied by the trickling streams as the sun disappeared behind the backdrop of mountains.

Chapter 10

THE WEDDING CARS pulled off the causeway, parking on the beach by the shell of an old warehouse. A heron stood motionless in the shallow waters of the salt flats opposite. Not a ripple teased the waters of either bay as Spyros fussed to get the bridal procession ready to walk the last few hundred metres to the church, over the bridge which crossed the cutting connecting the bays of Korfos and Mirabello.

Men fumbled in their pockets for cigarettes as the guests formed groups happily chatting, content not to be corralled. All went quiet when Popi stepped from her car. Katerina, who had travelled alongside her, disguised her tears by hugging her close. How much she had missed her daughter and Crete. It was hard to imagine a place more sublime and Popi more than matched the beauty of her surroundings as her classic white dress was revealed.

Spyros sensed his moment and, with all eyes being on Popi and her mother, managed to herd the guests who were to make up the traditional bride's party into a loose group. Popi and Katerina dabbed at each other's eyes with tissues as the arresting sound of a bow drawn across the strings of a lyra signalled it was time for the procession to be on its way.

From somewhere in the group, out stepped the musician; and Popi stared for a moment, surprised to see it was a young woman. Walking towards the cobbled bridge over the canal, the lyra player improvised, sometimes resting the instrument under her chin like a violin, other times suspending it in mid-air in her left hand, letting the bow bounce off the strings. Tourists walking out towards Kalidon stopped to clap the procession as it passed by.

On the bridge Popi and Katerina stopped. Looking up into the mountains they saw the small village where they had lived as a family all those years ago. Lowering their gaze they looked out into the distance to the familiar view of Spinalonga, along the waters of Korfos to the canal and out into the bay of Mirabello.

Katerina gave Popi's hand a squeeze, bringing them back to the present. Winding their way between the two disused windmills, they walked beside the canal towards the small chapel of Analipsi. Memories flooded Popi's mind as she took in the beauty of the whitewashed church. Briefly she allowed herself to recall the day

182

her father told her she was leaving for England. She touched a hand to her throat and the necklace of Britomartis.

Looking at her mother, Popi smiled. She could not remember the last time she had seen her mum so happy. She could not have been more excited that Katerina had travelled to Crete for the wedding, the first time she had stepped foot on the island since the traumatic break-up of her marriage. Somewhere behind them in the procession was Andrew, dressed in a traditional Scottish kilt and sporran, the man who had done so much to help Katerina rediscover happiness. But there was something else. Seeing her mother now, Popi recognised how relaxed she seemed. This was her world; where she was meant to be.

An altar had been set up in the parched courtyard, illuminated by the light bouncing off the bright cream walls of the chapel. Groups of guests stood among the meagre grass that eked a living in the churchyard. Others sought shade under the palms. Men sat smoking on the low stone wall, beyond which the inscrutable calm of the bay gave away no secrets of the sunken city which lay beneath.

The lone bell hung silent in its belfry, its rope secure against a window catch on the church wall. Spyros, who was acting as best man as well as master of ceremonies, took his place beside the altar where Costas waited, the groom handing Popi a bouquet as she approached.

'You look beautiful,' Costas whispered as she took the bunch of wild flowers gathered from the surrounding hills.

Before Popi could respond, the priest had begun the ceremony. The blessing of the rings, the passing of the crowns above the couple's heads and the traditional promenade around the church all went past in a flash. Popi felt as though she had not stopped smiling throughout the whole solemn proceeding. The bell rang out and gunshots were fired into the air, the lyra began to play and Spyros hurried around to try and cajole people back to the reception in town. Nobody was in any hurry to move. Flasks of raki emerged from the pockets of some guests with which to toast the happy couple. Katerina embraced her daughter before turning to hug Costas as Andrew popped the cork on a bottle of champagne.

Spyros knew when he was beaten and just let the celebrations take their natural course. Eventually the guests found their way back to the formal reception at a large taverna in Elounda. On the street outside, a traditional wedding dish of *gamopilafo* risotto of rice and goat broth was being stirred by a chef whilst a whole lamb roasted on a spit. Inside tables were laden with an array of mezzes and jugs of wine both red and white.

The young woman musician was now joined on the raised dais by two men. One took a lyra from its case, the other a guitar whilst the woman exchanged her lyra for a fiddle. As the band struck up, Costas led Popi to the floor for the traditional opening dance. As best man, Spyros was next to dance with the bride then, as Costas had no family, Popi tooks turns with Thea, her mother and Andrew.

As soon as empty dishes and jugs left the table they were replenished. Popi thought back to the day she had returned to the island following her father's death and how she had been worried that she would not know anyone. In no time her mother was welcomed by guests, eager to rekindle their old friendship. Andrew too was made to feel at home, Katerina laughing as her kilted boyfriend was swung around the dance floor by villagers wearing traditional Cretan dress.

As they ate, Popi and Katerina soon fell into deep conversation, daughter and mother confiding in each other for the first time in months. Popi apologised to her mother for not opening up to her before as she had been afraid to worry her. She explained about her rocky relationship with Costas and how the dramatic rescue at Turtle Beach had finally brought them together. Katerina was visibly touched when she heard Manolis had named the caique after her. Not willing to spoil Popi's happy day, she sniffed away a tear at the knowledge of how much her husband had truly loved her, even after the separation. Looking out towards the dance floor at the man she now loved, she smiled to think of where the twists and turns in life had taken her.

Costas circulated among the guests with a new-found confidence. Basking in their well wishes, he could not remember a time when he had felt this sense of belonging. If the future was as yet unsure, he knew that with Popi by his side they could face any challenges which life might throw at them. Now the caique was finished he would need to find work and until his new wife began her tours on the boat there was no way they could gauge how successful they might be. But such concerns were for another day, for the moment he just basked in his happiness.

It was midnight before the first guests began to leave and the early hours before the happy couple were driven home to Popi's house in the village. Katerina and Andrew were to stay at Spyros and Thea's cottage, and still buzzing with the events of the day they stayed up on the terrace talking.

It was mid-morning by the time Spyros' phone rang, letting him know the couple were ready for their agreed lift down to the harbour where they were to go off on the new caique for a couple of days alone. Loading their stash bags of clothes and food in the back of the truck, they set off on the short journey down the mountainside. The bay below glinted, its surface like a looking glass filled with a promise which reflected the happiness of the young couple.

As Spyros parked in a spot near his boat, Popi and Costas turned to each other, shock registered on both their faces. The berth where their caique should have been moored lay empty. Spyros was unable to keep a straight face for long.

'Come with me, I have a surprise for you.'

Popi's uncle grabbed their bags from the back of the truck and headed off towards the coast road in the direction of Plaka.

'Look, there she is!' Popi pointed ahead to the jetty near the Old Boatyard taverna where *Katerina* was moored. From her mast flew a flag announcing 'Just Married' and the rigging was dressed in blue and white bunting.

'She's beautiful, thank you uncle.' Laughing, the couple hurried towards the caique, not noticing Spyros stopping outside the taverna. Turning they saw him ripping a For Sale sign off the wall at the same time as the closed shutters were thrown open to reveal Katerina, Andrew and Thea sitting at a table laid for a champagne breakfast.

'I hope you're not in too much of a rush to enjoy a small celebratory meal before you go?'

'That would be lovely. But what is going on?' Popi asked. Costas smiled nervously. What were his new family doing in his uncle's taverna? He felt uncomfortable at the thought of being in a place which held such bad memories for him.

Looking about her now, Popi could see a kiosk on the roadside by the taverna, newly painted to announce 'Boat Tours – Underwater Safaris, Stars and Legends Cruises'.

Popi's smile could not get any wider. 'You did all this?' she gushed. Thank you, uncle, it's brilliant!' Spyros was still holding the For Sale sign he had torn from the wall.

'Come inside, you two. Let's have something to eat and I can explain.

They sat at the table and a waiter brought plates of fruit, cheese pies, boiled eggs, yoghurt and honey as the champagne corks popped and Spyros revealed his secret.

'I have started a new business. In fact, if we are all in agreement, I hope to be entering into several new family partnerships.'

'I have bought the lease to the taverna. For some reason Christos disappeared after the episode on the beach and the lease was put up for sale. The restaurant will no longer be called The Old Boatyard. With your agreement, Costa, it will be renamed The Boatyard.'

Costas followed Spyros' eyes to the side of the taverna opposite the kiosk. He hadn't noticed the bright new tarpaulin erected at the side of the building.

'I would like to start a boatbuilding business with you, if you will have me as a partner?'

Costas could not believe what he was hearing. He had never been so happy in his life. Yesterday he had married the woman of his dreams and now he was being offered the chance to run his own business, doing what he had always wanted to do.

'Thank you Spyros. Thank you so much. The answer is yes, I would love to become your partner.' Costas wasted no time in agreeing, shaking Spyros' hand as glasses were raised, toasting the start of the new venture.

'I think there is something else you should hear about.' Spyros turned to Katerina. 'Shall I tell them or will you?'

Katerina could hardly wait; she was raring to reveal to her daughter her life-changing news.

'We have decided, Andrew and I, that we are coming to live here on Crete. Spyros has kindly offered us a partnership in the taverna and a place to stay with him and Thea until we find our feet.'

Popi stood and hugged her mother. Overflowing with joy, she could not remember a moment in her life which had been more blissful.

When she let her mother go, they all sat down and Katerina explained how they had come to that decision. She told Popi how she had missed her and had worried when she had heard that she was staying on in Crete. She had kept in regular contact with Spyros and Thea to make sure that her daughter was alright. Missing her, and with the uncertainty surrounding European nationals in Britain, she and Andrew had decided to consider a fresh start. He was nearing 55-years-old and could draw his pension from then.

'Returning here convinced me how much I had missed being home. Just stepping off the plane at Heraklion made me feel in some way complete again. Spyros had made us the offer of running the taverna. But until we got here for your wedding I was not sure. Now I know I have never been more certain of anything in my life.'

The late breakfast ran into lunch as the family made plans for the future. Now the taverna would no longer be boycotted by the locals, Spyros was sure that in such a perfect spot it would make money. Costas now had somewhere he could work, maintaining the local boats, and who knows, someday a new boat might be commissioned. He could also work with Popi, crewing aboard the caique.

The last boats were making their way home from Spinalonga as the newly-married couple stepped aboard *Katerina* and cast off its lines. Waved off by their family on the quay, Popi and Costas stood either side of the tiller, steering their way toward the channel seawards with the gentlest movement of their hips. The sun was still warm and the scent of thyme, sage and wild garlic blew in on the breeze from the island of Kalidon. The moon had already risen, tentatively sharing the sky with the setting sun. Popi reached to switch on the navigation lights as they set a course through the northern channel past Spinalonga.

The night air was still warm as they hugged the coastline. Not a breath of wind wrinkled the alluring face of the sea. Above the stars shone like celestial buoys lighting the way to eternity. A shooting star shot across the sky. In that moment Popi and Costas felt the comfort of being two small people together on the face of the earth. Hugging each other they said nothing, steering the boat by instinct towards the place they both knew they were heading.

Behind them *Katerina* drew a light thread of foam across the waters, the slightest of links to where they had come from. The mountains cast a dark shadow over the sea, the only sign of life the headlights of a solitary car threading its way around the bends. In that moment Popi thought back to how far she had come since her father died in the early spring. Now it was autumn and in those 6 months her life had changed beyond compare. She was married, had a house in her true home and a future doing something she loved. Costas too had found something he had been searching for since he was a child. He had found love, the security of a family and the chance to follow in the tradition of a craft which went back to Minoan times. Beneath the vastness of the starlit skies both Popi and Costas could feel their place on earth.

In the darkness they could not see the chapel on the hill but could sail close enough inshore in the calm waters to spot the entrance to the cove. Neither of them had returned since the day of the accident but both pondered how such near tragedy had brought them to this happiness.

Popi throttled back on the engine as they passed through the narrow entrance to the cove and Costas went forward to dive in and swim the bowline ashore. Popi dropped an anchor astern. Tomorrow they would dive and try to retrieve the grapple and chain that had been abandoned in the storm.

As Costas swam back to the boat, Popi stripped off and joined him in the warm sea. Night swimming beneath the stars, the sprinkled glitter of phosphorescence glowed in the water. Back aboard they dried off before pouring drinks and sitting talking in the cockpit. Going below, the only motion of the boat was the gentle rocking as they made love in the cabin in the forepeak.

Not wanting to let the moment go, the couple were too happy for sleep. Pulling on fleeces against the slight chill in the night air they returned above deck and lay in each other's arms staring up at the sky. The half-moon, now bright illuminated the beach, the tamarisk-fringed patch of sand dwarfed by the backdrop of mountains rearing up behind it.

'Look,' Popi whispered, pointing.

Where the breath of water met the beach, a shimmer of phosphorescence dotted the surface. Another followed, and then more lights dusting the shoreline.

Staring overboard, the couple could just make out the forms of the baby loggerhead turtles making their bid for freedom, heading for the safety of the seaweed beds that clung to the headlands cradling the bay. Those that survived, when grown would head for the open sea. When mature, the females would make the long journey back to this same beach to lay their eggs.

'Good luck, little turtles,' breathed Popi. 'I hope you find your way home.'

Did You Enjoy this Book?

If you liked reading this book and have time, any review on www.amazon.com or amazon.co.uk would be appreciated. My website *Notes from Greece* is https://notesfromgreece.com, and it would be good to meet up with any readers on my facebook page at www.facebook.com/richardclarkbooks.

Made in the USA
Columbia, SC
09 March 2020